IN SHADOWED DREAMS

A NOVELLA

S. Judith Bernstein

Published 2023 by Trickster Cat Publishing LLC

IN SHADOWED DREAMS

For more information please contact
https://www.trickstercatpublishing.com/contact

Library of Congress Cataloging-in-Publication Data is available

ISBN 978-1-959825-00-5 (paperback)
ISBN 978-1-959825-01-2 (ebook)

For My Dragons,

for always being the Alex to my infuriating Raven.

I could not have written this without you.

*"A word is dead when it is said, some say.
I say it has just begun to live that day."*

EMILY DICKINSON

PROLOGUE

"We need allies." Liza was pacing again. The dark red long slitted skirt flowed around her as her bare feet beat indents into the soft carpet of the small library reading room. "We can't do this on our own! Grace and Charlotte are on their way, but it's not enough and we're nearly out of time!"

She spun on her heels, fast enough that her dark brown hair whipped out behind her as she continued leaving markings in the antique rug.

"I think . . . I think I know someone who could help us."

Liza spun on her heels again, this time coming to a complete stop, staring at Alex where he sat hunched over in his armchair, his elbows on his knees and his head in his hands.

"You know another awake mage?"

And you didn't tell me. She didn't say the second part of her thought out loud but she might as well have.

"Not exactly. I mean, I know two, but they're not very strong and they're both trying to let it go . . ."

Liza's shoulders slumped.

"Then . . .?"

Alex reached into his pocket, pulled out his phone, and stared down at the lock screen.

"Lorie's not a mage . . . not exactly . . ."

Curious, Liza padded over to stare down at Alex's phone. His lock screen was a photo of two people laughing with their arms around each other's shoulders. Alex was immediately recognizable—short brown hair standing up in the back in untidy spikes, and brown eyes shining with amusement. The other inhabitant of the photo was a girl. She had dyed-black wavy hair streaked with silver and black eyes that, even in photograph, seemed slightly unnerving somehow.

"Is that Lorie?" Liza asked quietly. She wasn't quite sure what was going on with Alex, but she could tell that something about this Lorie person was a very sensitive subject for him.

Alex shook his head. "That's Raven." He shook his head again. "That *was* Raven." He sighed. "I guess, in a sense, it's Lorie now."

"I see . . ." She didn't, but it was clear that Alex had cared deeply about this Raven and that, one way or another, she was no longer a part of his life. Liza wasn't sure whether she should be pushing him or not, so she settled for trying to bring him back to the topic at hand.

"So, this Lorie isn't a mage then?"

Alex shook his head.

"He's a hitman, a really good one."

Liza blinked, then she blinked again.

"A. Hit. Man." She spoke the words slowly, enunciating every syllable, as though she was trying to find some secondary meaning within them.

Alex nodded. "Have you ever read *Shadows of the Silver Towers* by A. B. Levinson?"

Liza shook her head.

"It's an ongoing series of crime dramas. Lorie is, that is, the protagonist is a hitman who goes by the name 'Lawrence Rain.'"

Liza blinked a third time.

"So this Lorie is just a fictional character?"

Alex sighed. "Not anymore."

This time Liza didn't blink; she just stared. "What?"

Alex took a breath, then shakily let it out.

"Did you hear about some unsolved murders that occurred in New York City about nine months ago?"

"Murders? In New York City? No. I'm from Massachusetts so I'm not really familiar with the goings-on in . . . Wait!" Liza paused midsentence, her eyes going wide as her mind finally caught up with her mouth. "About nine months ago? You mean the last incursion?"

Alex nodded.

"So that's how you were awakened and how you already knew about them?"

It wasn't really a question, but Alex nodded an affirmative anyway. Liza walked heavily to the armchair facing Alex's and sank into it.

"How did you survive?" she asked.

Alex opened his mouth to answer but she shook her head before he could speak.

"No, wait. You'd best tell me everything from the beginning."

Alex's eyes flickered from her back down to his phone's lock screen. He stared at it for a long moment before he raised his head again, nodded slightly, and began.

PART 1

THE SLEEPERS WAKE

(NOW)

"It was a complete coincidence. We were all just in the City to see a stupid movie. I mean it wasn't a bad movie but what were the odds? We didn't live in the city. Any other day we wouldn't have been there, but Raven was too impatient to wait till it came out on DVD, and it wasn't coming to theaters in the suburbs."

"We?"

"Me and Raven Colman and Sean Tyler and Ari Sarpa. The college in the suburbs where you found me, we all go there. Me and Sean and Ari were all juniors. I guess Raven was too. She used to be the year above us, but she had to take medical leave for a year because of her migraines. Anyway, it was an afternoon movie, and we were on the subway back to Grand Central that evening when things started to get weird . . ."

As they got onto the subway, Raven was talking every bit as enthusiastically as he Ari and Sean. The movie had been everything they had hoped it would be, and they'd been discussing it nonstop since the moment they left the theater. Sean and Raven were arguing about the symbolism of the colors used in one of the movie's most emotional scenes while Alex and Ari were still excitedly rehashing the fight choreography in another. But as the subway pulled away from the station, Raven became more and more quiet. Sean, who had joined in Alex and Ari's discussion of the movies action climax didn't seem to notice, but Alex did. It surprised and even worried him a little. These sorts of conversations were where Raven usually came to life, regurgitating dialog and details with an accuracy of memory that he could never match. He watched as she leaned forward, resting her elbows on her knees and pressing her eyes into the palms of her hands. Alex reached out, placing one hand lightly on her shoulder.

"You okay?" he asked.

Raven raised her head slightly and blinked fuzzily up at him.

"Headache," she murmured. "Gotta sleep."

He nodded. It happened with Raven sometimes.

"Do you need meds? Or do you want to put your earbuds in?" Sometimes when Raven wasn't feeling well she took her onset medication, but other times just spending a few minutes listening to an audiobook seemed to be enough to revive her. This time, however, Raven just shook her head slightly.

"No, sleep."

He nodded, even though she couldn't see him with her eyes once again buried in her hands.

"I'll wake you up when we get to our stop."

She grunted her thanks and her shoulders relaxed a bit. Alex shook his head in wonder. He would never be able to understand how she could just do that. Whether it was in a restaurant, in the dining hall, in class, or sitting on a crowded New York subway, when Raven decided it was time for a nap, she was just out. Shrugging to himself, Alex turned his attention back toward his other two friends who were now laughing over recollections of some of the movie's funniest moments. Alex joined in and he hadn't even realized how deeply immersed he was in the conversation until he felt a hand closing around his upper arm. He twisted, tense and startled, to see Raven standing over him, a wild look in her strange black eyes. He stared up at her, surprised. Raven was awake? When had that happened? Her naps usually ran pretty deep and he'd been expecting to have to start shaking her awake well before their stop, so why was she on her feet? They were just pulling up at a stop, but it wasn't theirs. Maybe she'd woken up and, still half asleep, mistaken their location.

"This isn't—" he started to say but Raven cut him off, her voice crisp and not at all sleep muddled.

"We have to go."

"What?" Sean asked. He and Ari were staring up at Raven too.

"Now!" Raven snapped.

She pulled Alex, who was too startled to resist, out of his seat and toward the now opening subway doors, shouldering her way roughly through the people who stood between her and the exit. Calling inquiries after her, Ari and Sean hurried to follow them. The four just barely made it off before the doors of the subway car slammed behind them, but Raven did not stop once they reached the platform. Still grasping Alex's arm, she dove down the subway tunnel, moving along the platform so fast that Alex and the others had to jog to keep up with her.

"Raven, what the hell!" Alex asked, finally getting his bearings enough to yank her to a stop. He was panting slightly, and when she spun to face him, Alex saw that she was too.

"We have to keep moving" she hissed. "We aren't safe here!"

"Aren't safe?" Ari asked, tensing, her hand sliding automatically into the pocket of her denim shorts, and Alex knew that she had her hand around her switchblade. Unlike the rest of them, Ari had grown up in a city. From what she'd said about it they'd gathered that while the neighborhood of Chicago that she was raised in wasn't the worst, it also wasn't the best. Ari knew about not being safe. The switchblade was proof of that. Regardless of where she was going or for how long or with whom, Ari never left campus without it. She had also, as far as Alex was aware anyway, never had cause to use it, or even draw it since coming to college, but he didn't blame her for taking the precaution.

Sean, however, had grown up in a lazy New York suburb and had no such instincts to be triggered by Raven's words.

"What the fuck do you mean not . . . !"

"Not here!" Raven interrupted him. She tugged on Alex's arm, trying to get him moving again. But before she could take more than a step, attempting to drag Alex behind her, another voice spoke from behind them.

"Well, well, what have we here?" it said in what Alex could only think of as a BBC accent.

They all whirled, Raven moving as fast as Ari, surprising Alex, considering that Raven was the least physically active of the group.

The man to whom the voice belonged was tall, wiry, dressed respectably, and appeared to be in his late twenties or maybe early thirties. A tourist maybe, or traveling businessman, not someone who should have had any interest in a few local college kids. That was when Alex noticed that they had come far enough down the tunnel that they were alone with the man. Perhaps it was just Raven's fear catching hold of him, but Alex felt a chill down his back. Usually Alex hated crowds. They were his least favorite part of coming into the city, worse even than the smell, but suddenly he found himself wishing that another train would pull up, flooding the platform with people.

The man walked slowly toward them, a satisfied smile lighting on his face as he approached, and Alex noticed a glint of silver as the light from one of the tunnel's few fluorescent bulbs caught on the brooch pinned on the man's left breast. It drew Alex's attention and he saw that the brooch, done entirely in silver, was of a sword standing half in and half out of a pool of water. There was something about the brooch that fascinated him, something that drew his eyes to it, something beyond just the way it sparkled in the light, something . . .

"Who are you?" Sean's question broke the spell the brooch seemed to be weaving over Alex, and his eyes flicked from the man's pendant back to his face.

"Me? Nobody you need remember," the man replied, still moving calmly toward them.

"W-What do you want?" Alex asked, and he wasn't surprised to hear his voice shake a little. There was something about this man that terrified him.

"That should be obvious, little sleeper. Or is it sleepers?" the man asked, his eyes widening slightly as he focused briefly on them, first Ari, then Sean, before returning his gaze to Raven and Alex. "Yes, I can see that it must be. Well, well, isn't this a lucky find. Although, I am a bit curious how you knew to ru—"

The man stopped talking abruptly as Ari pulled her knife from her pocket and held it, low and ready, in his direction.

"I don't know who you are or what you want, but you're giving me the creeps. I suggest you back the fuck off before I call the police."

"Now, now," said the man, coming to a stop and raising his hands in what seemed to be a placating gesture, although Alex noticed that the man was still smiling the same satisfied smile. "We wouldn't want to do anything hasty."

The man's left hand began to tilt sideways and suddenly Alex felt Raven tense, her hand tightening convulsively around his arm. He felt a slight warmth in the air around him, like a current somehow connecting him to the man. Then Raven released his arm and leapt forward, faster than he'd ever seen her move, so that she was standing between Ari and the man, left arm flung out as though to shield her friend. The wrist and fingers of Raven's open left hand twisted until her fingers were pressed together closed. There was something oddly familiar about her movements, like Alex had seen them somewhere, but before he could place them a loose brick, lying by one of the subway tunnel's walls, flew through the air at Ari's head as though of its own volition. It stopped abruptly as though it had crashed against something just before it could pass through the space directly above Raven's outstretched arm. The air against which it had seemingly collided rippled like water and flickers of light traveled along it, and then the brick was rebounding backward. The man tried to dodge it but he wasn't fast enough. It collided with his shoulder and he fell to the ground, cursing in some language Alex couldn't identify.

That was when Alex recognized what he was seeing. It was a scene from the movie they had just watched . . . well, sort of. The location and characters had been different and the thing repulsed by the shield had been a battleax, not a brick, but the shield had been the same, so had the ricochet, and so had the way that Raven moved. And it was all completely impossible.

"What the . . . what the hell!" Ari sounded completely unnerved and just a bit panicky. In other words, she sounded exactly how Alex felt. A thousand thoughts were rushing through his head at once, most of them some variation of "Did I actually just see what I thought I saw?" and "Is this real?" but one traitorous corner of his mind murmured another question: "Does this mean that magic is real?"

They were all staring at Raven, trying to process what they'd just seen. For her part, Raven hadn't spared them a glance. All her attention was fixed on the man lying on the tunnel floor and clutching his shoulder. He had ceased to curse and was just glaring up at them, panting from a mixture of pain and rage. Then the man's hand dropped away from his injury. Alex saw torn fabric and blood, but that wasn't what grabbed his attention, neither was the way the man pressed both of his hands against the tunnel floor. What caught Alex's attention was the sudden sensation of heat once again tingling along his skin. It was coming from the man. He knew it. He couldn't have explained how he knew; he simply did and with that knowledge came something else: the need to act.

He lunged forward, grabbing Raven by the shoulders and dragging her sidewise toward Ari. Less than half a second later, loose rocks and pebbles from all along the tunnel sliced through the spot where Raven had been standing, coming so close to her as Alex pulled her away that one of the pebbles grazed her cheek in passing, leaving behind a thin line of blood.

The combined sounds of the rocks hitting the ground just past where Raven had been and Sean swearing as they clattered to the floor directly in front of him nearly drowned out the man's next words, spoken not to them but to his sword brooch against which the fingers of his injured arm were now pressed. Alex could just make out the words "two awake" and "backup" over the clatter of stones. Alex tensed, and he could tell by the sound of Raven's muttered "blast" that she had heard as well.

Raven stepped away from him, her hands brushing together then moving outward to the sides, fingers rotating inward. A shadow seemed to move with her like there was another figure with shoulder-length black hair standing with her, and Alex knew what was going to happen, even if it was impossible. Raven had moved just like a character from the movie and, just like in the movie, metal began to move. Bits of scrap and rusted-off bits of track and drainpipe flew through the air, glowing the red of newly forged steel, coalescing in front of Raven into a thin staff with leaf-bladed ends. All Alex could do was stare, as fiction became reality before his eyes. He was so caught up in what he was seeing that he barely noticed the way that his skin warmed in response to Raven's power. Then a new heat prickled through his feet and the ground began to shake. For a wild moment Alex thought that the next train must finally have arrived to save them, but a second later he realized that it was the platform, and not the tracks, that was in motion.

Alex stumbled sideways, fighting for balance. He saw, out of the corner of his eye, Ari lose her balance and Sean grab her arm to keep her on her feet. Raven also stumbled but she did it forward, toward the man, raising the staff she now held as she went. Then she was bringing it down on his head. The man gasped once, crumpling backward, and everything stilled.

For a few moments they all just stood there, panting and gasping and staring at the respectably dressed English man lying on the subway platform floor in front of Raven.

"Is he dead?" Sean's voice was shaking.

Raven shook her head dazedly, letting the staff fall from her hands with a clatter. "Just stunned, I think." She took a shaking breath, seeming to collect herself. "We have to keep moving; we aren't safe here."

This time none of them questioned her.
They just ran.

"We ran for as long as we could, up out of the subway and down the street, pushing people out of our way as we went. We didn't stop till Raven fell against a wall."

"Fell?"

"Yeah. Like I said, she was the most out of shape of us, plus she must have been tired from using all that magic."

Liza nodded. "You must have been as well."

Alex looked up at her sharply, then, slowly, he nodded.

(31 MONTHS BEFORE)

"If you're looking for more fantasy novels, you won't find them."

Alex jumped; he'd been so busy glaring at the bookcase in front of him that he hadn't heard the person, whoever they were, coming up behind him. He glanced over his shoulder and his eyes were caught in strange black orbs. He blinked. The orbs, eyes, belonged to a person with wavy hair in a shade of black, that, judging by the dark brown of their eyebrows and lashes, probably wasn't natural, and highlighted with silver streaks that were definitely out of a bottle. They were slim and small, dressed in dark denim shorts and a black "the future is accessible" T-shirt. They were leaning back against the bookcase behind him, staring down at him with an amused smile and an oddly intense look in those curious dark eyes.

"Huh? But the sign says sci-fi and fantasy." He gestured at the small plaque at the end of the aisle which did, indeed, say "Science Fiction and Fantasy."

They clicked their tongue and a look of irritation slid briefly across their face.

"The librarians don't know much about fantasy. A little bit of it ends up here where it should be, but the rest ends up split between 'Children's' and 'YA.' Sometimes a series even ends up split between all three." They rolled their eyes.

"Oh." Alex sat back on his heels and stared up at them. "That's stupid."

"Yep." They crossed their arms. "What book are you looking for anyway?"

"*Inkdeath*, by Cornelia Funke."

"Ah." Their eyes lit up, and they gave a slight nod of approval. "They put that one in Children's. I'll show you."

They pushed themself away from the bookcase, starting for the end of the aisle and gesturing for him to follow.

"Um, sure. Thanks."

As Alex scrambled to his feet, they glanced back at him over their shoulder.

"I'm Raven. She/her. Sophomore. And you're a freshman." It wasn't a question.

"That obvious?"

"Yep." She smiled slightly, as though enjoying some sort of private joke.

"Great. And Alex, he/him."

"Alex." She nodded slightly, dark eyes fixing on him again with strange intensity for a moment before she turned back toward the end of the aisle and started walking.

"What the hell!"

Alex was still panting for breath, but Ari appeared to be breathing just fine.

"What the hell was that?" She glared at Raven, who was leaning against a nearby wall, her hands on her knees.

"Tell me that we imagined that! Just tell me!" Sean was shaking.

Raven glanced up at him, blowing a strand of wavy black and silver hair out of her face. She was still gasping for breath; yet when she spoke her voice was calm.

"You're not. I feel like it should be pretty obvious by now, but this is the part where I tell you that magic's real." She smiled a little, seemingly amused by the looks that they were giving her. "Come on," her smile grew, "you shouldn't have such a hard time with this; you're all mages too."

"We're what?" Sean spluttered.

Ari shook her head slowly, disbelieving. All Alex could do was think about the sensation of heat and how it had flowed through him, and how he had understood it instinctively. As impossible as it all was, with the memory of that warmth still lingering under his skin, how could he doubt it? Raven slid down the wall until she was sitting against it.

"Right. Since we need to rest anyway, let's do this. Welcome to magic 101. Class is now in session."

"Is this a joke to you?" Sean snapped.

Alex reached out and put a hand on his friend's shoulder. Raven glanced up at them.

"Look, do you want answers or not?"

Sean glanced back at Alex, then sighed, shoulders relaxing slightly.

"Ok, talk."

"Magic is real." Raven began. "It's always been real, and it didn't stop being real when most people stopped believing in it. But it did lose some of its power. It's like in Peter Pan. You can't use magic unless you believe in it. But just because most people think magic's just a myth, it didn't stop people from being born with it—a decent number are. They have some power when they're kids, but the older they get the more they buy into the idea that magic's a myth so the less they can use it, until they can't use it at all. They are the Sleepers. Those with magic who don't know it and can't use it."

"So, if no one knows about magic then who was that man and what the hell are you?" Ari sounded somewhere between curious and accusatory.

"I'm the exception. I'm a see-er. Those of us born with the sight are always at least partly awake. Typically, it takes seeing another mage work magic to fully believe in magic enough to use it. It's a matter of proof, but we come with our proof built in. When I see something in dreams and then it happens, I can't help but know that magic's real."

And Alex remembered. He remembered all the times that Raven had just put her head down in the middle of the day and how she often woke mumbling but with a strange light in her eyes.

"That's how you knew," he said it quietly, but they all turned to look at him. Sean and Ari blankly, and Raven with a slight nod of approval. "Raven dozed off on the train," he told the other two, then turned back to her. "You saw it, didn't you? You saw that man come after us."

She nodded again.

"Wait." Sean looked honestly confused. "Then why have us get *off* the train?"

"There were two men in our subway car. They were going to come after us as soon as we left the train, but we moved fast enough that they didn't have time to get off."

"But who are they?" Ari sounded as lost and confused as Alex felt. "Why are they after us?"

"I only know what I saw, and images aren't always clear, but basically this time it was a warning. It seems that in some parts of the world, such as England, there are cults that have raised their kids to keep magic alive from generation to generation so they can use it. Only now they want more power, and they've figured out how to capture the magic from dead mages, and they decided that the number of people from all different backgrounds in Manhattan makes it a good hunting ground." She smiled grimly. "Welcome to the hunting ground."

"Huh?"

"Just a quote."

At some point Ari had seated herself, arms crossed, against the wall opposite Raven, but now she rose and began to pace. "So basically these Brits are running around the city looking for anyone who feels like magic and trying to kill them as part of their generic evil villain plan to get more magic, and since you're a fucking prophet or something, they decided that you'd make a great non-rechargeable battery?"

"Not quite." Raven turned back to Ari. "It's true that the more asleep someone is, the harder it is to sense that they even have magic. Most of the city's sleepers should be safe enough. That's why they're going to hunt down the few awake mages they find with everything they've got."

"K, great, so they're extra special after you then?"

"Like I said"—Raven shook her head—"magic is real."

"Yeah, I got that part."

"Exactly."

Alex felt a sinking sensation in the pit of his stomach as a knot of dread coiled itself there. Suddenly he was very much afraid that he had picked up on exactly what Ari was missing.

"That's the problem." He said it softly and the other three turned to look at him. Ari and Sean sharply, and Raven with a small smile of approval.

"What?" Sean asked and Raven answered before Alex could.

"Magic is real. You said it, you saw it, which means you believe it, and since you were sleepers, that means you're now awake. In other words, they're not hunting *me*; they're hunting *us*."

It was Sean who broke the ensuing silence with the words that they had all been thinking. "We've got to get the hell out of the city!"

Liza whistled. "A see-er. No wonder you guys made it out. Most of the other active mages who were on the island that day didn't get out before the barrier went up and, after it did, well, they couldn't defend themselves . . ."

"We didn't."

"Huh?" Liza blinked at Alex.

"We didn't make it out before the barrier went up either. For all I know things had been going on all day or even all week. Raven only saw that we were in danger when the danger was right in front of us. By the time we were running for Grand Central the barrier was already going up."

"Then how . . . ?" Liza trailed off suddenly, remembering that this story was a tragedy, at least in some respect, and that Raven, it seemed, had never gotten out at all.

"Raven," he said simply, looking back down at the lock screen of his phone, and Liza noticed that Alex's fingers had gone white from clutching it as he talked. "I said how much Raven loved stories. Her magic fed off them, like what she did in the tunnel."

Liza whistled again. "That's one hell of a power." *Not that it would have done her any good once the barrier went up,* Liza thought but didn't say.

"Exactly." Alex nodded slowly, and Liza got the feeling that he was responding more to her thought than to what she had said aloud.

He looked back up at her. "We tried to head for Grand Central as fast as we could, but another guy with one of those pendants found us. Ari spotted him from far enough away that we had time to run, but we still got pretty far off course trying to lose him."

(31 MONTHS BEFORE)

As it transpired, *Inkdeath* had indeed ended up in the children's section. Raven took him right to the very shelf, pausing only long enough to ask if he'd read it before. When he told her that he had, she began to ask him about his thoughts on the development of the character Dustfinger. That prompted a conversation which lasted them out of the children's section, through the checkout line, and across the green to the dining hall for lunch. At some point during lunch, Alex commented on how Raven had known exactly where to find the book he was after and Raven had nodded and told him, "I probably know the library's fantasy section better than the librarians do. Sci-fi and mystery, too, of course."

"I take it you spend a lot of time there."

She snorted at his understatement. "Just a bit."

"So what other stuff are you involved with?"

She shrugged. "I go to Hillel sometimes. That's about it."

"You're not in any clubs?"

She shook her head. "Too antisocial, too much of an introvert." She smiled, making it half a joke.

He raised his eyebrows. "You're being social enough with me."

She froze for a moment, her expression turning serious, eyes focusing again on his with sudden intensity. For a moment she looked as though she was on the verge of saying something but then she relaxed back against her chair, the smile returning to her lips. She shrugged, as though half to dispel the last of her tension, half in response to his comment.

"Well, you like the right books."

(THEN)

They were leaning against the brick wall of a narrow side street, taking another much-needed breather, when Sean asked the question, "So, what are the odds that we all turned out to be mages anyway?" He'd meant it to be rhetorical, but Raven answered almost immediately, "Oh, it wasn't a coincidence."

The other three rounded on her, and she looked back at them calmly. "How do you think I picked you?"

"Picked us?" There was something slightly dangerous in Ari's voice. Raven nodded, seemingly unperturbed by the change in her tone.

"Right. I've never actually met another awake mage, at least not till today, but I'm pretty okay at sensing sleepers. That's how I found all of you. With you two"—she nodded at Sean and Ari—"the feeling wasn't super strong, but it was enough to get me to look twice at you, and once I did I realized I liked hanging out with you guys. Alex, though . . . Alex stood out the moment I met him. He's the most awake sleeper I'd ever found, so I was curious." She turned her head so that she was looking straight at Alex as she spoke. "I knew I had to get close to you, find out how your mind worked, if having magic meant that you thought about the world differently or that your brain was wired differently, the way mine is."

Alex stared at her in disbelief. His heart, which had been slowing as they rested, beginning to pound again. "So that's why," he managed to splutter out, "that's why you started talking to me, started spending time with me?"

Raven nodded. "Exactly. I have to admit I was fascinated by you. Truth be told, I still am."

Alex didn't know what to say to that. Anger was boiling up inside of him, washing away the fear that had been knotted so tightly in his stomach. A thousand disparate memories raced through his head, memories of all the time they'd spent together, all the things they'd done, all the moments they'd shared. He knew in a general way that he was trying to recontextualize the images, trying to see them through this new lens, but the only thought that actually managed to come together inside his mind was *I thought we were friends, best friends . . .*

"That's messed up." Again, it was Sean who broke the silence. "All this time you've just been using him?"

"Well, I wouldn't call it—"

"Then, what would you call it!" Alex cut her off, his voice cracking with sudden fury.

"Enough!" Ari snapped, raising a hand in each of their directions. "You've got enough breath to fight, you've got enough breath to run. We need to go."

Alex shot Raven a venomous look before nodding at Ari. "You're right; let's get to Grand Central." *And,* he thought to himself, glancing back toward Raven again, *once we get there, I'm never speaking to you again.*

They had only gone a few more blocks when Sean and Raven both began to slow. Sean was shivering, and Raven was pinching her temples the way she did when she had a migraine coming on. At that moment Alex didn't give a damn about Raven's pain but he slowed anyway, worried about Sean.

"What's wrong?"

Sean shook his head, wrapping his arms around himself as though trying to hold in the shivers that were steadily getting worse.

"The warmth, it's going, leaving, I . . . ," he trailed off, frowning in confusion. "It's like there's some warmth always all around us. I didn't notice it before but now that it's leaving, I can feel where it isn't."

Alex stared at him; the heat that Sean was describing sounded like and yet unlike the prickling heat that Alex had been feeling every time someone around him used magic. Now that he thought of that heat though, he noticed that it too seemed to be shifting. As they'd run, he'd begun to notice it drifting off of Raven, and, to a lesser extent, off of Ari and Sean, but now it felt as though it was pulling back, drifting away from him and his friends in a way that felt utterly and intuitively wrong. Alex licked his lips nervously. In front of him Sean was still shaking, and beside him Ari had begun to sweat.

Raven took a few steps backward, half stumbling into the wall behind her, and slid down it into a crouch, her hand still pinching her brows.

"Just give me a minute," she murmured.

Alex opened his mouth to object, but Ari raised a hand to silence him. He blinked and then he remembered the subway and what Raven had told them about being sighted. He nodded curtly to Ari, acknowledging that she was right, that they needed to give Raven this moment. Still the concession burned in him; it burned to do anything to help her now, burned like her words had as they seared themselves into his brain and like the heat of magic that was slowly wafting its way out of him, only to be replaced by the heat of anger. He hated it, hated everything about it. He hated the magic, hated it for being the thing that Raven prized most about him, the reason she'd decided to spend time with him, the only part of him she seemed to value. He began to shake but, unlike Sean, Alex's shaking had nothing to do with magic.

Sean leaned himself against the wall a few feet away from Raven, as though he wasn't sure whether or not he really wanted to be near her either. They had all been hurt by Raven's words.

"So that was when the barrier started to go up?"

Alex nodded. "I could feel it. I didn't know what I was feeling, but I could feel it. Ari too, although Sean felt it more than either of us. I guess he's more attuned to whatever magic it was they were using to put up the barrier. Go figure. Anyway, we stayed like that for a while, waiting for Raven to get whatever it was out of her system. The whole time, all I could do was think about how mad I was at her, how I thought I hated her." Alex's voice cracked on the last words and his fist clenched convulsively around his phone. Liza saw tears in his eyes, but before she could decide whether or not to say anything about it, he continued.

"Raven?"

A muffled response from within. He opened the door and peered into the darkness beyond, eyes blinking to adjust.

"Hey, I wanted to come by and see how you're doing, and I brought you some food. Do you mind if I co—"

"Come in or stay out, but don't stand in the doorway! You're letting in the light!"

"Sorry."

Quickly Alex stepped into the room, letting the door swing shut behind him and promptly tripping over something in the dark.

"Damn!"

"Careful!"

Trying to be just that, Alex felt his way across the dorm room to the bed.

"Here, I brought you dinner."

He held out the sandwich with one hand and pulled the smoothie from where he'd been holding it, pressed between his arm and body, with the other. It was blueberry, Raven's favorite.

He was starting to be able to see things now and could make out the shape of Raven lying sprawled on her back in the bed staring straight ahead of her, her head unmoving even when she reached toward him to take the sandwich.

"Thanks." She said it in a much softer voice, softer not only than her irritated tones of a moment before but also than her normal speaking voice. She sounded weak, exhausted, as though she had been completely burned out.

"It's bad?"

"Yep." She gave a sigh, part frustration part resignation. "I feel like someone's boring a hole through my right eye, and the left isn't much better."

"Is there anything you can take? I mean"—he grimaced to himself at how utterly obtuse that had sounded—"are your onset meds helping at all?"

"Not really. After I eat I'm going to take some sleeping meds and try to knock myself out so I don't have to deal with it, but that's about all I can do."

"Ah . . ." He wasn't sure quite what else to say to that. "Feel better" would have sounded hollow and "Good idea" might have come off as condescending, especially after that last blunder. Then he realized that she hadn't taken the smoothie, so he held it out toward her again.

"Here."

"What is it?"

"A smoothie."

"You stopped at the café?"

"Yeah, I know you often like cold drinks so . . ."

"But the café's not covered by the meal plan . . ."

"I'd noticed."

"Thanks, Alex, I mean it. Thank you."

(THEN)

Raven's eyes snapped open and she leaped to her feet, stumbling forward as though she was still half asleep and had moved too fast. Instinctively, Alex moved to grab her arm and steady her, as he had done so many times before. She shot him a grateful look, and he looked away, releasing her arm as anger and hurt once again washed over him. Raven leaned backward until her shoulders were resting against the wall behind her.

"We're in trouble." When she spoke, her voice cracked as though her tongue was still in the process of waking up, and there was a layer of hurt in her tone that Alex did not want to think about.

"I saw it. They're putting up a, a . . ." She hesitated, licking dry lips.

"Barrier. It's a barrier." They all swung around to stare at Sean. He shook his head, bewildered. "I don't know how I know that; I can just . . . feel it. It's there, growing . . ." He gestured vaguely.

Raven nodded slowly. "Yes, they're putting up a barrier. I saw it."

She shivered.

"A barrier?" Ari spoke slowly, and there was danger in her tone. "You mean like to keep us in the city?"

Sean shook his head. "I think . . . I think it's worse"

"Worse? What could be . . ."

"They're shutting down magic." Raven's voice was crisp, but Alex could hear real fear in it.

"What?"

"I don't know how they're doing it; I don't know enough about magic to know, but they're putting up a barrier, and once they finish no one will be able to use magic on the island."

Ari frowned. "But wouldn't that affect them, too?"

Raven nodded. "We're not the only ones to use magic against them, so they decided to put a stop to this and hunt people down with conventional weapons, guns and knives and stuff. Most people who can use magic to protect themselves won't know how to defend themselves without it. And since we're four active mages together, they're definitely coming after us."

They all stared at Raven in horror.

"How long do we have?" Alex whispered.

"Not long. We need to move!" Raven took off running down the alley, and the others followed.

They had only gone two blocks when Sean stumbled, brushing past a couple businessmen to lean heavily against the outside of a shop window. The other three skidded to a halt, turning to look at Sean, who was shaking again. He shook his head, gasping for breath to speak. They were all exhausted from running, but Sean's exhaustion went beyond that. It seemed a response to the barrier rather than to anything he'd actually done.

"We're n-not . . . going to make it. I can tell. We only"—he paused to pant for breath—"a few minutes."

"We need to try to get as far as we can then!" Ari's hand went to her pocket, and Alex knew that it had closed around her knife again.

"No!" Raven shook her head, eyes wide and wild. "We need a plan, we need to use magic while we can, we need . . ." Her voice trailed away and she bit her lip, eyes defocusing.

"We don't have time for that!" Alex snapped. He extended a hand to Sean. "Come on, I'll help you."

Sean shot Alex a grateful look and took his hand. Alex tugged him away from the wall and they began to run again. At first Raven hung back, lost in thought, but as they neared the next corner, she sped up, racing past them with a burst of energy that Alex was astonished to see she still had.

"This way!" she shouted, throwing herself around the corner in a direction that led not toward Grand Central but in the direction of Central Park.

"What the . . . ?"

Ari shook her head and chased after Raven. Alex followed, pulling Sean with him. Raven looked back at them. "I need your knife!"

"The hell!" Ari snapped back.

"Knife!" Raven shouted again.

Briefly, Alex was very glad that the back alley Raven had turned down seemed to be mostly deserted. There was a homeless man dozing in a shuttered doorway, but other than that there was no one to be seen. If anyone else had heard Raven shout about a knife like that, they would probably have called the police. Just as briefly, Alex wondered if that would be the worst thing in the world, but then he immediately dismissed the idea. The police would see them as kids messing around and would either write them off or write them up. Either way, it would not help their current situation one bit.

Ari cursed under her breath, but something about the urgency in Raven's voice got through to her because she put her head down and quickened her pace, fumbling in her pocket for her knife as she ran. Raven slowed her mad dash long enough for Ari to cram the closed switchblade into Raven's fingers. Then Raven was off again, running flat out for the park, Ari in hot pursuit, Alex and Sean trailing behind, and darkness closing in all around them.

As she ran, Raven flipped open the knife and slashed it across her arm. Alex choked and nearly stumbled as he saw the flash of the blade and glimpsed a line of crimson following the knife. What the hell? Then Raven turned, just a little, just her head, slowing as little as possible, and their eyes met. He wanted her to see the anger he was feeling written across his expression but he was completely distracted by the look in her eyes. Raven's strange bird-black eyes, usually so remote, were burning with some strong emotion that he didn't have time to identify before she turned away from him again and raised her now bloodied forearm to her mouth. Then Alex had to blink rapidly because the air in front of him seemed to blur and double as he felt heat build around her. The world cleared again and Raven stumbled for a moment. Alex thought that she would fall, but she managed to get her feet back under her and keep going, if at a much slower pace than before. Her gait had also changed, her movements becoming jerky and off kilter, and Alex wondered if she'd twisted an ankle when she'd stumbled.

He was at the point of calling to her to demand to know what the hell she thought she was up to when her rapidly slowing pace brought her abreast of Ari, and the latter grabbed her arm, dragging both of them to a complete stop. Raven stumbled again, half pulling away from Ari, forcing Ari to grab her again to keep Raven upright. Alex sped up, trying to catch up with them to find out what was happening when he felt a tug on his hand and was dragged up short by Sean who stumbled to a halt, half falling forward. Alex grabbed Sean's forearm, keeping his friend upright, and the world blurred around him again. Again, Alex tried to blink it back into focus, but this time when the world came back some of the colors seemed to have gone from it. Everything seemed a little grayer and, somehow, a little sadder as well.

"The barrier." Sean's voice was hoarse. "The barrier is up."

"Fuck!"

Alex turned to see that Ari and Raven had come jogging back. Despite everything else going on around them, Alex still registered surprise. Raven never used ordinary profanity, preferring instead to adopt the curses of her favorite novels. However, Alex supposed, if this wasn't a time for profanity, he didn't know what was.

Ari nodded. "Fuck indeed."

"We've got to get to the train station," Sean murmured.

"Right," Ari said. "And we'd be a lot closer by now if someone hadn't decided to run off in the wrong direction." She rounded, glaring, on Raven. "Are you going to tell us what the hell that was about?"

"No."

Alex turned to glare at her as well. "Fine! Keep your secrets! But next time you decide to run off and risk your life, don't drag us with you!"

Raven shrugged. "You didn't have to come."

Alex decided that he hated her.

"Come on," Sean said wearily. "Let's go."

There didn't seem to be much to say after that as they all turned and trudged off back in the direction of the train station, too tired to move at anything faster than a walk. As they passed the mouth of a narrow alley, however, Raven paused. She stared at it for a moment, then nodded to herself and turned down it, beckoning the others to follow.

"Where are you going now?" Sean demanded.

"I know a shortcut," Raven called back over her shoulder.

"And you just expect us to follow you again?" Alex snapped.

Raven shrugged. "Fine, don't come then." She kept walking. They all glared after her for a few moments. Then Sean and Ari shrugged, and the three of them followed.

"We'd gone down a few twisting back alleys, walking still, heading back in the general direction of Grand Central, when we heard running footsteps coming from an alley that intersected ours just up ahead. We all froze, except Raven, who took two more steps forward and to the side before she stopped as well."

Alex paused.

"Were they?" Liza asked gently.

Alex nodded, shuttering.

"They were. There were two of them. They had guns, with silencers and everything. I'd never even seen one in real life

before, and there they were. They were pointing them at us, and I
. . . I just stood there; I didn't know what else to do."

Ari took half a step forward, as though she was trying to
get in front of the others to shield them. Her hand was back in her
pocket and Alex knew that she was reaching for her knife again,
probably more out of habit then because she thought it would do
her any real good. She didn't have it though. Raven did.

Raven.

She took two more steps forward and to the side before
she froze as well. Her hands were in the pockets of her sweatshirt,
mirroring Ari's, and Alex realized that one of them must be
around the knife. One of the men said something to the other but
Alex couldn't hear it over the pounding of his heart.

"They pointed their guns at the three of us, and all I could
think was that I was dead."

"The three of you?"

Alex nodded. "Raven was off to the side. All of those
sideways steps she took. They couldn't really cover all of us at
once and I guess they didn't see her as a threat, at least not
compared to the rest of us. Raven's this skinny girl, just five one."
He gestured with a hand, indicating her height. "The silver streaks
make her look a little older—maybe that's why she does it—but
even with them . . . she's the oldest of us but she looks like the
youngest. Ari's five seven." and an athlete, and I'm an inch taller
than she is, and Sean's two inches taller than me with broader
shoulders. If they were going to decide to not bother with one of
us right away it was going to be Raven. With the three of us

IN SHADOWED DREAMS

standing together and all, I guess they just decided to kill her after . . ." Alex shook his head. "I mean hell, without her magic even I would have said Raven was the least dangerous one."

"I take it that wasn't the case?"

"Not even close." There was no pleasure in the way Alex said it.

When Raven moved she was still holding her body strangely, yet, with the part of his brain that was still remarking on trivialities, Alex noticed that there was also something weirdly fast and fluid about her motion. Still it took him a moment to fully process that she had moved at all, and he wasn't the only one caught off guard. Of the four of them, Raven was closest to the gunmen, yet her extra steps had been perfectly judged to place her far enough to the side that she was just beyond their direct line of sight. By the time the gunmen realized their mistake, she had already closed the gap completely.

Raven lunged for the wrist of the gunman nearest her, and it looked to Alex as though she was trying to grab the gun away from him. Alex's eyes registered a glint, as though the solitary streetlamp had caught briefly on the metal between Raven's fingers, and then she was holding the gun and the gunman was hunched over his wrist, cursing, and there was blood flowing from between his fingers. It was all over so quickly that not until later was Alex able to fully realize what must have happened. Raven had been holding Ari's knife in the hand farther from Alex and it was the opening of the switchblade which had caught in the streetlight. Raven had grabbed for the gun with her near hand and, without the slightest hesitation, she had used the other to bring the knife down across the inside of the gunman's wrist. Before Alex could figure out how it had gotten into her left hand, Raven was slamming the back of the gun into the gunman's face with all of her strength. Her blow caught him on the left side of his forehead, so that he stumbled right, straight into his companion, who was just aiming his own gun at Raven. Then, before he could push his stunned companion away from him, Raven raised her own gun and pulled the trigger.

"She . . . shot him." Alex's voice sounded tired, empty, as though he was still numb from the shock of it. "Killed him. It wasn't loud because of the silencer, but I could still hear it. The force of it jerked her arm back. Not enough to do any damage to the arm but enough for her to swear and rub her shoulder, although she didn't drop the gun. It was almost like she'd known to expect the recoil but had misjudged it somehow . . ."

His voice faded away then suddenly he slammed his fist into his leg. "I'm such an idiot! I should have seen it right then! I should have realized!"

"Realized what?"

Alex shook his head. "I was so busy being mad at her, hating her even, that I didn't see what was right there! I'd never seen anyone killed in front of me, and it had me pretty shaken up, but what messed me up even more was the fact that Raven didn't seem to be messed up at all by it, and she was the one who'd just killed a man for the first time. I started asking myself if it really was the first time, and what I really knew about her anyway. I mean I thought I knew her pretty well, but the Raven I knew could never have done something like that. Even after the fight in the subway tunnel she reacted more like I thought she would. She kept it together while it was happening, but she still seemed pretty freaked out. That time she had only stunned the guy, but she was still as shaken up as the rest of us.

"But there they were. The three of them. The dead man, and the one she'd pistol-whipped who was still stunned or unconscious or something. And Raven, standing over them and clearly more upset about the fact that she'd strained her arm on the recoil than about actually shooting someone. And I started asking myself if I'd ever known her at all really. If maybe she had killed people before and done other horrible stuff and really had just been interested in me as a sort of observational science project. If maybe she'd actually been messed up in this stuff before and had just been lying to us about the whole 'cult coming after innocent people' thing and they were really just after her and she'd just decided to drag us all down with her."

Alex let out a long breath. "I was such an idiot."

Liza tried to come up with something comforting to say in reply, but she still didn't quite get the whole situation, at least not the part that Alex had been missing, so she decided to just give him a moment. He stared down at his knees for a minute, clearly lost in morose thoughts. Then, without raising his head, Alex sighed and continued.

Alex, Sean, and Ari just stood there for a moment, frozen by shock and horror. Then Raven turned back around to face them, and Alex took an involuntary step backward. There was blood on her sweatshirt. The sweatshirt was red, so it didn't stand out much, especially in that dimness. If he had been any farther away or not paying attention, he wouldn't have noticed it at all, but he did. There was blood on both of Raven's hands, too. Her left sleeve was still rolled up from when she had sliced her arm open with Ari's knife. Alex was still wondering why she had done that, but it wasn't a particularly deep cut, and the bleeding had stopped a while before. Still, it left a trail of blood all down

Raven's arm and the outside of her wrist and thumb. Her right hand had a few drops of blood on it as well, spattered there when she had slashed the gunman's wrist. With her black eyes and hair, she looked like something out of a horror movie. Beside him he could hear Sean retching, but to Alex the blood wasn't the worst part of it. The worst part was just how calm she looked, like she was just on her way home after a movie, or on her way to class.

The look didn't belong at a crime scene, or on a murderer.

Raven bent down and picked up Ari's knife from beside the man she had attacked with it. He was conscious, curled up, and moaning on the ground, trying to hold his bleeding wrist and the rapidly swelling side of his face at the same time. Looking at him, all Alex could think was that at least she hadn't killed him too.

(11 MONTHS BEFORE)

The screen door banged open as a couple of children slammed through it, darting across the porch and down the creaky front steps to pelt across a front yard still littered with last autumn's pine needles. Alex watched them go, slightly bemused by the fact that they had just raced right past him, a stranger on their front porch, without a second glance.

"So I see you met hurricane Sella."

Alex turned back to the screen door to find that it had been pushed half open again and that Raven now stood leaning against it, her arms crossed and her wavy black and silver hair for once pulled back in a braid. It made her look younger, and Alex wondered briefly if that was why she didn't pull it back more often. It looked nice.

"Sella?"

"Simon and Ella."

Alex glanced back at where the two were racing, barefoot, toward the tree line.

"Don't all those twigs and stuff hurt their feet?"

Raven shrugged. "Not that they'll admit to. You need a hand with your stuff?"

Alex shook his head and gestured down at the rolling suitcase sitting at his feet. "It's just this and my backpack."

"All right." She pushed the screen door fully open and gestured for him to follow her inside.

The door opened onto a kitchen and dining area on his right, the two separated by a granite-topped peninsula jutting out from the wall. On his left was an area that seemed to serve as a mud room, complete with a hall closet and a variety of winter boots, none of which appeared to be part of a matching set. Beyond the dining area was a door, and beyond that a narrow flight of steps and a living room with another exterior door on the far end. Raven waved him into the living room and gestured for him to sit on one of its two threadbare sofas.

"You want something to eat or drink?"

"Um, nah, I'm good for now, thanks."

"Probably a good thing. It's grocery shopping day so we're pretty low on food anyway. My aunt's at the store now, though, so will be restocked in time for dinner."

"Ah."

The silence that followed felt slightly awkward, as though this new environment had robbed them of their usually easy flow of conversation.

"How was the drive?"

"Fine. Pretty. I've never been this far upstate before."

"Yeah, it's nice up here. Cold in the winters though."

"I'll bet."

Another uncomfortable silence. Alex turned to look at Raven. She seemed to have a thing for propping up doors because she was leaning, arms folded, in the doorway to the living room just as she had been at the front door a few moments before. The same body language, the same forced casualness, the same uneasy tension hidden just below the surface. It occurred to him briefly that she'd been standing just like that against the bookcases on the day they'd met, too.

"How are you?"

She shrugged, pushing herself away from the doorframe and moving to drop onto the other couch.

"Resting. More or less. I read, I watch the brats, I go to doctors. I'm on another new med now, propranolol. It's a beta blocker, a heart med, but it's been shown to help with migraines, so they figured it was worth a try."

He waited. Silent.

She shrugged again. "It's medical leave; it's not supposed to be exciting."

"Where will wants not a way open, so they say—"

"And so I have found myself." She finished the quote automatically then smiled a little. "Fair enough and it has given me time to read and watch stuff. Speaking of, have you finished watching *The Librarians* yet?"

"No, I've only just finished season three."

"We should do that. Put your stuff upstairs and I'll get the TV set up?"

"Sure."

"You sure you don't want anything to drink at least?"

"How about some orange juice, if you have it?"

Raven nodded. "Got it. My room's the first one up the stairs to the left. I put an air mattress on the floor for you."

Alex nodded, gathering up his backpack and rollie suitcase and heading for the staircase. Raven also stood and headed back toward the kitchen. Halfway to the door, however, she turned and walked back toward him. Raven caught him at the bottom of the steps and put her arms around him.

"I missed you."

"Yeah, you too."

(THEN)

"We should go." Raven said as she wiped the knife on her sweatshirt before dropping it back into her pocket. "Before this one"—she nodded at the moaning man—"feels the need to try getting up."

Raven lifted the left side of her sweatshirt and made to tuck the gun into the waistband of her black skirt. Then she stopped, frowning down at it as though trying to figure out if she could somehow wedge it so that the elastic waistband would hold it in place.

"Are you serious?" Ari's voice came out cracked and half strangled. "Are you fucking serious?"

Raven looked up from trying to stow the gun and shrugged.

"What? Are you mad that I killed him? Because if I hadn't they would have killed us. You should know that better than anyone, Ari."

Ari's mouth snapped shut and she stepped over to Sean, putting a hand on his back as he straightened up and wiped his mouth with the back of his hand.

"Fine," Alex said bitterly. He nearly spat the words at her. "Let's go."

"We went. We didn't really talk, and we walked since we weren't in any shape to run. It went on like that till we started hearing voices and seeing people walking past again, and I realized that we'd made it almost to Times Square."

"We should split up," Raven said.

The crowds were growing thicker and the lights were growing brighter. They'd paused for a moment in the doorway of a closed shop to take a breath and regroup. Or, at least Ari had announced that they were taking the break, and Sean and Alex had been all too willing to go along with her. None of them had asked Raven. None of them were even looking at her. Alex had half expected her to complain about the halt, or even to go right on walking without them, but she hadn't said a word. Alex was a little sorry that she hadn't decided to keep going. He thought that if she had, there was a very low chance that any of them would have gone after her or made any effort to call her back.

Raven's was the first to speak since Ari proposed the halt, and her words came as enough of a surprise that three of them actually turned to stare at her

"Abandoning us?" Ari asked acidly.

"No." Raven's voice, was calm, seemingly unbothered by the accusation. "But we're going to need to cross through the area around Times Square in a minute. Even at night it's crowded, and I think I can hear some sort of concert coming from there. It'll be impossible to navigate. To stay together, we'll have to slow down a lot, and even if we do, we'll probably still get split up at least a couple of times. Then we'll waste more time trying to find each other and all the while one of us would be alone in the middle of a crowd meaning that the cultists could come from anywhere around us, and we wouldn't have a clue. If we split up, however, we can hold hands as we go, still move pretty fast, make it harder for them to track us, and still meet up on the other side. Sean's still a mess from vomiting and from the barrier going up, and Ari can handle herself in a fight, so you two should stick together and I'll stick with Alex."

"Now, wait just a . . . !" Sean spluttered. It was clear that he wasn't thrilled about being insulted by someone who'd just committed murder, but then his eyes flicked to Alex and he realized that was only half of it. Sean was worried about letting him go off alone with a killer, especially one who had clearly upset Alex pretty badly.

"You can't just take him and run off like that!"

"Why not?" Raven stepped into Sean's personal space and smiled up at him. "You jealous?"

Alex stared at Raven, frozen momentarily by a sudden impossible idea.

Sean turned slightly red and started to splutter something about that not being what he meant, but before he could get more than a couple words out, Alex cut him off.

"Fine, let's do it." He snapped out in a tone gone hard and urgent.

He grabbed Raven's wrist, ignoring the now mostly dry blood, and began to drag her away from the other two.

"What the . . . ! Alex?" Ari called after them.

"We'll meet you on the other side!" Alex shot back, his heart pounding.

"Wait! Alex!" Sean shouted, but Alex ignored him.

Alex sighed and shook his head.

"All I could think was that I needed to get her away from them as fast as possible."

"What, why?" Liza asked. She was genuinely confused this time. Raven might have been acting strange, might have proven to be colder and more pragmatic than any of her friends could wish, but she hadn't actually done anything to intentionally put any of them in harm's way. In fact, every violent thing that she had done that night seemed to have been to protect them as much as herself.

"Do you still not get it?"

"No."

Alex sighed again. "It was so obvious."

Liza could tell that the frustration in his voice was still all for himself, not for her, so it didn't bother her.

(6 MONTHS BEFORE)

". . . So then I told him that 'no, it doesn't seem reasonable, since students who don't need large print don't have to scan their own readings in order to have them in electronic format, so why should I?'"

Sean laughed, "You didn't!"

"I did! And he didn't really have an answer for that, so he's going to do it, but I think he hates me now. Raven, you saw the look on his face."

Sean laughed again, Alex joining in this time, but Raven remained unresponsive, just staring out of the window.

"Raven?"

"Huh?"

"You saw his face, right?"

"Saw whose?"

"Professor Hunt's, after that argument we had after class . . . Oh, never mind." Ari rolled her eyes. "Anyway, I'm just glad this is the last semester I'm going to have to take class with him, and I'm pretty sure he is too!"

Alex and Sean laughed again but Raven's only reaction was to begin twining and untwining her fingers, still staring out the window.

"You okay?" Sean asked, frowning slightly in her direction.

"Huh? Yeah, fine." Her eyes flicked toward him then back toward the window. Abruptly she jumped to her feet and began pacing back and forth across the small study room they had co-opted.

"What's up with her?" Ari asked, one eyebrow raised.

Sean shrugged, clearly as mystified as Ari was.

"She can still hear you, you know." Raven's tone was impatient.

Ari raised her hands in a gesture that was half placating and half defensive. "Well, that's news to me, considering you didn't when I was talking to you a minute ago."

Raven paused for a moment, giving Ari a small, apologetic smile. "Oh. Sorry 'bout that." Then she returned to pacing.

Ari caught Sean's eye and he shrugged again. Alex frowned at Raven thoughtfully.

"You've been getting twitchier and twitchier all wee—"

"What are you reading?" Alex's question cut Ari off midsentence.

She looked slightly taken aback by his interruption but not bothered, as Raven came to a sudden halt, her head jerking up and her strange dark eyes fixing on Alex.

"What?" Sean sounded as surprised by Alex's question as the other two looked.

"You finished *Tinker Tailor Soldier Spy* a week ago," Alex said slowly, continuing to speak directly to Raven. "You read the latest *Kingdom* chapter four days ago, and we're not due for another chapter of *Arslan* for another week and a half. I know you're between shows at the moment because you were complaining about it yesterday and I haven't seen you carrying a book around since you finished *Tinker Tailor*, so what are you reading?"

"Well, I was going to reread the sequel, *Smiley's People*, but it's still checked out for another two days and I already reread the prequel I like, so . . ."

"So you haven't read or watched anything for days," Sean concluded.

Ari rolled her eyes. "I should've realized. You're always impossible when you're between books. Let me guess, you haven't been sleeping again either."

Raven shrugged.

"You know you could try reading something else," Alex suggested.

"Like what?"

"Um, I don't know. You've been doing murder mysteries a lot lately, right? How about some Dorothy L. Sayers or Agatha Christie?"

She shrugged again. "Maybe." Then, turning toward the door, "I'm going to go check and see if *Smiley's People* came back early." She pushed open the door, and they all watched as it swung shut behind her.

"Do you worry about her sometimes?" Ari asked.

Sean snorted in amusement. Alex's lips twitched as well, but as the other two turned back toward their homework, Alex was typing "Books like *Tinker Tailor Soldier Spy*" into his computer's search bar.

(THEN)

Alex dragged Raven with him around the nearest corner, turning in a direction that actually had them heading farther from Times Square, back in the direction of quieter streets, but not Grand Central. At that moment though Alex didn't particularly care, and if Raven minded, she didn't appear to see a need to do anything about it. She just let Alex drag her along without complaint. It was probably a good thing, too. Alex's heart was pounding fit to burst, and if she'd resisted, Alex honestly wasn't sure what he would have done.

Then Alex saw what he'd been looking for. The mouth of an empty-looking small, dark alley, just on the far side of a closed parking garage. He yanked Raven around the corner into the alley, pulling her far enough down it that he figured they'd be out of sight from the street. Then he released her wrist, spun around, and slammed her against the wall of the alley, pinning her against it by her forearms, leaving her no chance, he hoped, to go for either Ari's knife or her stolen gun.

"Now!" His voice came out sharp and furious, somewhere between a whisper and a shout. "Who the hell are you, and what the fuck have you done with Raven?"

Liza stared at Alex blankly. "What the . . . ?"

Alex was shaking. "It wasn't even her. All that time, and I couldn't even see that it wasn't even her!"

Liza put up one hand in a warding gesture, an automatic reaction to his sudden shout. "Alex, I don't . . . What made you think?"

Alex took a breath, visibly struggling to get himself back under control before continuing in a more normal tone.

"It was what she said to Sean that tipped me off. The signs were there long before that, of course, but it took such a stupidly obvious mistake for me to see it."

"Mistake?"

"She . . ." Alex actually appeared to be having trouble working his tongue around his next words. "She *flirted* with him."

Liza blinked. Then she blinked again. Then she blinked again. The only thing she could think to say was "No, not really."

"I mean, I guess technically." She continued hastily, seeing the look on Alex's face. "She did imply that he might be jealous about her going off alone with you, another guy, and at the same time that there might be something between you two to be jealous of, but from the way you made it sound, it all sounded very automatic, just a ploy to get Sean to stop objecting. It didn't sound like Raven actually meant anything by it."

Alex nodded. "Exactly. Raven would never have done that."

"Why not? It's not like people don't say things like that all the time, even just as friendly teasing . . ."

"But not Raven." Alex's voice was crisp with certainty. "Never Raven."

"Why?" Liza sounded as puzzled as she felt.

"Because Raven's Aro Ace, Aromantic Asexual. Some people who are still flirt anyway, but Raven doesn't, not ever. She wouldn't be comfortable. I'm not saying she couldn't do it if she needed to for some reason but *never* as an automatic first response. It was just so completely out of character for her that it really made me stop and *think*. Before, I'd been so busy being mad at her for being cold and not really caring about any of us, about me, that every time she did something strange, I just decided to hate her a bit more without really thinking about whether there was a chance that something else was going on. But when she said something, something so un-Raven like, it caught me up short for long enough that I *did* think, did ask myself what could possibly be going on with her, and once I did, the evidence was everywhere."

"The way she killed that man you mean?"

"Well, yes, there was that, the way she killed him without hesitating even a moment, like she'd done it a dozen times before, but that was just the most obvious one. There was the way she attacked them. I'd never seen her move like that, and Raven's not athletic. The way she was moving all wrong, as though there was something wrong with her balance. At first I thought she'd just twisted an ankle or something, but that wasn't really right. It was more like, all of a sudden, she wasn't sure how to handle her body weight. There was the way she expected the recoil from the gun, like she was used to handling them and knew what to expect from that model, but still misjudged it, but only a little, not badly enough to do any real damage. Again, as though her body wasn't quite what she was used to. There was the way she kept stepping forward when the rest of us froze, so that she ended up in the gunmen's blind spot, like she knew exactly what she was doing. Even the way she started cursing and the way she seemed confused by her own clothes. And I remembered the look she gave me right before all the weirdness started with her, just before she used Ari's knife to cut her arm open to cast what I assume was some kind of spell . . ."

Liza let out a low whistle. "If it were just two or even three of those things, I would have told you that it could just have been coincidences, but taken all together I'm starting to see what you mean . . . And, it's not like you'd be telling me about it this way if you'd been wrong."

Alex nodded. "Exactly. That's why I had to get Raven, to get whoever it was, away from the others as fast as possible once I realized. We were alone with an unknown killer, and, whoever they were, unlike Raven, they had no reason not to turn on us."

(4 MONTHS BEFORE)

"Why that sharding ve-vied be-blasted!"

"I take it the meeting didn't go well?"

"No." Ari's voice was thick with sarcasm. "It went fine; she's just cursing for the fun of it."

Sean rolled his eyes. Raven ignored them both as she continued moving away from the campus's main administrative building at a pace that could only be described as "storming," still cursing all the while.

"Shards and shells and Farenth's bloody egg!"

"What even are those curses?"

"Pernease." When Raven didn't pause long enough to reply to that remark either, Alex provided the answer.

He and Sean had been waiting outside the administrative building since they had decided that Raven couldn't reasonably bring all three of them with her to the meeting, and of them they'd decided that Ari's cutting bluntness would be of the greatest assistance.

"Pernease isn't a language," Ari snapped.

"I never said it was." Alex's reply was mild. He figured that the level of irritation in Ari's voice had less to do with him misrepresenting a detail of one of her favorite novels then it did the meeting that she and Raven had just left.

"Pernease, as in from the planet Pern. So Alex is right and right again when he said he didn't imply it was a language."

All three of them turned to face Raven, surprised that she had stopped both her moving and her literary variety cursing, and even more surprised to find that she'd actually been paying attention to their discussion.

Ari rolled her eyes. "Fine, fine."

"So," Sean asked looking from Raven to Ari, "are one of you going to tell us what happened in there?"

"What always happens! They don't give a damn!" Raven's fists worked in pent-up frustration.

"Seriously?" Alex let out a disgusted breath.

Sean looked to Ari for confirmation.

Ari nodded. "That pretty much sums it up."

"Accommodation!" Raven was shaking now, and Alex could see the upset and, yes, fear, hiding just behind the anger. "They call this accommodation! What the hell do they expect me to do? Preschedule my absences? That's not how migraines work!'

Alex hesitated for a moment then stepped forward and put an arm around her shoulders. Raven leaned forward against his shoulder and suddenly began to cry. Alex wasn't sure quite what to say but he hastily wrapped his free arm around her, pulling her into a hug. Sean and Ari stepped up beside them, patting her shoulders.

"We'll figure it out," Ari murmured.

Alex nodded. "Yeah, what Ari said, and you're tough. You'll get through this. You always do."

(THEN)

'Raven' stared calmly up at Alex as though they, whoever they really were, weren't particularly bothered by being slammed up against the wall of a dark alley by someone bigger and stronger. Yet, Alex could feel a tension in their arms that belied their seeming relaxation.

"Well?"

They blinked up at him through Raven's eyes, then smiled slightly.

"So you can tell? I was wondering when you'd finally catch on."

Alex let out a long, shaky breath, and his hands tightened convulsively on the stranger's arms. It was one thing to suspect, even to be sure, but another thing entirely to hear it confirmed. The stranger's smile grew, as though amused by Alex's obvious distress.

"Who the hell are you? And how the fuck did you, did you . . ."

"Take over Raven's body?"

"How?" Alex realized that his voice, his whole body, was shaking.

"I'm Lorie, Lawrence Rain, and as for the other, it's simple really. She gave it to me."

Lawrence Rain. The name was vaguely familiar, but Alex couldn't place it.

"What do you mean 'gave it to you'?"

"Just what I said."

Alex's nails were digging into Raven's—Lorie's—arms, but the stranger didn't seem to care.

"Where the hell did you even come from?" Alex's voice cracked on the last word.

Lorie laughed. "You really don't know, do you? She didn't remember you as clueless."

Alex glared.

"Have you ever read *Shadows of the Silver Towers*? No, I see you haven't."

"What?" Thrown off by the unexpected question, Alex was about to reply angrily, then when Lorie's words fully processed. Alex froze.

Shadows of the Silver Towers was one of Raven's favorite book series. A set of crime drama-cum-action-cum-mystery novels. He'd never actually read them, but she'd talked about them and, because of her prodding, they'd actually been on his list of things to read that upcoming summer. A new book—he believed it had been the fifth—had come out about a month earlier, and Raven had all but disappeared for the two days it took her to read through it. He wasn't sure she'd slept, and she'd been rereading and talking about the series ever since. It was the story of a hitman who traveled around the world to war zones and big cities for work.

The hitman's name was Lawrence Rain.

Alex felt his eyes widening in disbelief. All he could do was stare. There was no way . . . there was no way . . . Some part of Alex had to admit it made a twisted sort of sense, but there was just no way . . . His face must have shown his consternation because Lorie began to laugh. Alex's hands tightened convulsively on Lorie's arms, his nails digging into Lorie's skin, but again, Lorie didn't particularly seem to care.

"How?" His voice came out cracked and shrill, and he realized he was shaking.

It was too much; it was all too much. Over the course of the last few hours, everything in his life had changed too many times. Magic was real. He and his friends were being chased through New York City by evil British cultists who wanted to kill them. One of his closest friends wasn't actually his friend and was actually some sort of future-seeing witch who was just hanging out with him as some sort of science experiment. He'd watched someone who he thought was that friend kill a man in cold blood right in front of him, and only now it turned out that friend had actually been possessed by some fictional assassin.

It was all too damn much.

"Her stunt with the knife. Didn't you ever wonder what that was about? Magic was going down, and she didn't figure she'd make it out, so she handed over her body to me because she knew I'd use it better. And, I am."

"Undo it." Alex's hands were trembling, and he realized that if he didn't get a grip on himself, then he'd lose his grip on Lorie.

"Huh?"

"Undo it. I don't know how a fucking fictional character managed to possess Raven, but undo it."

Lorie let out a snort of laughter and Alex felt his blood burn. The guy was nothing more than fiction, just an author's words mixed with magic and illusion, but Alex couldn't help it. He decided to hate him.

"Really? Your life's in danger and that's the first thing you ask? Even when I'm your best shot at not getting shot? You really are like him." He smiled again. "No can't do. This body's mine now."

Like who? It didn't matter. Alex's fingers tightened convulsively on Lorie's arms again, his nails digging into the other's arms.

"Undo it!"

"Careful now. Wouldn't want to hurt Raven, now, would you?"

Alex swore. What the hell was he doing anyway? Raven was gone, there was some fictional creation sitting in her body, and the whole world had turned upside down. His shoulders slumped. Suddenly he felt exhausted. He stepped back, his hands falling away from Lorie's—Raven's—arms.

Lorie smiled slightly, raising his hands to rub at the places where Alex's nails had dug into his arms just below the rolled-up sleeves of his sweatshirt.

"Ready to go then?"

Alex nodded, too exhausted to even bother with an answer. Lorie grabbed his arm and began pulling Alex toward the entrance of the alley.

As the crowds grew around them again, Lorie kept a tight hold on Alex's arm, dragging him quickly toward Times Square. Always as he moved, he clung to the shadows around the bases of buildings, doing what he could to stay out of direct light, and Alex assumed he was trying to conceal the blood stains on his clothes, although Alex doubted that they were noticeable enough to catch the eye of a New Yorker. As the lights of billboards brightened the sky around them and Alex was jostled by crowds on every side, he began considering simply yanking his wrist from Lorie's hand and making his way to the station on his own. He didn't even know why Lorie was bothering to drag Alex with him, since Lorie could probably have moved faster on his own and had no reason to give a damn about him anyway. Besides, if Alex was right and Raven was more of a target than he was, then getting away from Lorie was the smart thing to do.

"It was a stupid plan." Alex sighed. "Hell, it wasn't really a plan at all, just me being stupid. It's not like I was thinking enough to call it a plan."

"That's understandable though. I mean you'd been through a lot."

Alex snorted. "Now that's an understatement," and Liza was glad to hear that a little of the amusement had returned to his voice. "Lorie had pulled me most of the way to the edges of Times Square at that point, and when he pulled me against a shop just outside of the flow of traffic, I decided to make my move."

"Finally, spring!" Alex lay back, stretching out half in the grass and half on the old towel that they were using as a blanket. It was the first truly warm day they'd had, and the green appeared to be celebrating by suddenly sprouting masses of both wildflowers and college students.

"Finally," Sean agreed, dumping his backpack beside Alex and dropping to the ground beside it. Ari waved them a lazy greeting with one slim brown hand while she took a bite of the ice-cream sandwich she held in the other. Briefly, Alex wondered where she'd gotten it from and whether there might be more where it came from, but obtaining one would probably involve getting up, and that sounded like just too much work at the moment. He decided to ask later.

Raven had also looked up long enough to give them both a quick smile in greeting before she returned her attention to the book she was reading. Ari's eyes followed Raven's.

"Did you start back at the beginning again?"

Raven nodded distractedly.

"How far are you through it this time?"

Instead of answering outright, Raven responded by beginning to read aloud. "It was raining the next time that Lorie saw the stranger . . ."

The famous London fog had rolled in and rolled back out again, leaving behind it a seemingly endless downpour. Lorie pulled his fists deeper into the sleeves of his sweatshirt and attempted to stifle a sneeze. The chill, wet air was getting to him and the bus

shelter where he sat wasn't insulated, but it would be worth it. He hoped. He was still annoyed about the last time, when the strange man had stepped right into his perfect line of sight, and the time before that when the very same stranger had taken his target by the arm and led him into a coffee shop just before he could pass by the alley where Lorie was waiting, and the time before that when . . . At this point Lorie was starting to wonder if the man was a bodyguard. At first he had taken him for a business associate, but the uncanny way that the man always seemed to move the target out of Lorie's way just in time was beginning to seem highly suspicious.

At the very least, the stranger's constant interference, intentional or not, was earning him Lorie's deep dislike, since he was managing to make the job far more complicated than it should have been. Lorie's target was one Justen Crants, a part-time bartender and full-time drug smuggler, whom the client, a wealthy businessman, had been laundering money for. The businessman had not been too clear about why he wanted to be rid of his sometimes associate, but from what he had, or rather hadn't, said, Lorie assumed that blackmail was involved. When Lorie had taken the job, he'd supposed, based on the businessman's description and his own—rather more thorough—research into Crants, that it should be fairly simple to catch the man en route to or from his bar and away from his underworld cronies. It would have been, too, if the stranger didn't keep popping up like a badly wound jack-in-the-box and ruining every trap Lorie set.

Oh, it wasn't like Lorie couldn't get a sight on Crants other times, but there was locating his target and there was locating his target at a time when he wasn't surrounded by civilians, and whenever Lorie thought that he'd finally achieved the latter, there the stranger was again. At this point Lorie had decided that his only option was to attempt to take Crants out while he visited one of his hideouts, something far more time-consuming—and more dangerous—than the quick job which Lorie had initially had in mind. For one thing, Lorie had realized in his first hour of watching Crants that the man was far too careful for Lorie to just follow him back to his bolt-hole without being noticed. For another, if Crants ever suspected that he was being followed, even once, he'd probably start changing his patterns of behavior in ways that would make Lorie's life far more annoying. Yet while this might mean that following Crants himself was off the table, the same was not true for some of his less scrupulous employees. Which was why Lorie had spent the last half hour sitting in a wet, cold London bus shelter waiting for a street corner drug deal to go down. Yes, Lorie had ample reason to dislike the stranger.

Attempting to swallow both his irritation and another sneeze, Lorie peered through one of the glass walls that had made the bus shelter the most sensible of observation posts, even if it wasn't the most comfortable. There were two men on the street corner now. One, who appeared to be some sort of petty official, was probably the customer, while the other, a man generically called 'Smith,' was Lorie's new secondary target. Lorie tensed but stayed put. Don't move yet, he told himself, a glass wall is see-through in both directions. Any sudden movements and they might just start wondering why it is you're still here even though the bus just pulled away.

Lorie's thoughts were suddenly interrupted by a sight of something flashing in the corner of his eye. He reacted before he could think better of it, whipping both his head and torso around, responding instinctively to what he knew could only be the flash of a camera. It was the stranger. Of course, it was the stranger, the same strange man who had guided Crants into the coffee shop and consistently ended up between Lorie and the perfect shot. He was slim with close-cropped brown hair, and his jeans and white button-down were wet enough to prove that he had been standing out there for a while now, although definitely not in his current position or Lorie would have noticed him much sooner. Wherever he had come from, he was now leaning against a lamppost just beyond the bus shelter, a small camera which Lorie recognized as being of a very expensive waterproof variety, in his hands.

Lorie's eyes widened. A camera, not a phone. An actual camera. Most people snapping shots of an illegal drug deal would have used their phone, far less conspicuous, far more convenient. The only reason not to was if the photographer was worried about the quality of his shot. Quality didn't matter if you just wanted the photo as evidence, either for the courts or for blackmail. The only time when quality was important was if the photographer expected the photo to be repeatedly viewed, enlarged, printed, and . . . The man was a reporter, (and a damn fool one. The lamppost's no kind of cover, and if I noticed the flash going off, then it's only a matter of time till his targets do too.)

There was a cry from behind him and Lorie spun back around on his bench to see that the two had, yes, noticed the unwanted attention they were getting, although whether it was the flash of the bulb or Lorie's sudden movements that had caught their eyes, he couldn't be sure. Whichever one it had been, though, it was the reporter they were noticing now and the reporter that they had begun running toward, and Lorie had no illusions about what would happen to the man if they caught up with him.

Lorie glanced behind him, expecting to see the reporter pelting away from there as fast as he could go, but to his utter incredulity, Lorie saw that no, he wasn't running; no, he hadn't even moved. Instead, the idiot just continued to stand there, snapping away with his camera as though his life wasn't in danger.

"Fuck!" The expletive left Lorie's mouth even as he was leaping to his feet. If the reporter ran off, the other two would run after him and for Lorie it would just mean another irritating missed opportunity and trying again on a different day. However, if they actually caught up with the fool journalist in front of or near the bus shelter, then one way or another, Lorie knew he'd end up being *dragged into the ensuing fight, even if it was just because the petty official would be nervous about eyewitnesses. At this point there was just no help for it, and if that was the case . . .*

"Run, you idiot!" Lorie shouted as he lunged forward, grabbing the journalist by the forearm and dragging him down the street, away from his—now their—pursuers.

—From Book 1 of *Shadows of the Silver Towers* by A. B. Levinson

(THEN)

Every time Lorie and Alex reached the side of another building where crowds were light enough to let them pause for a second, Lorie would stop just long enough to glance around and see if they were being followed. As Lorie was turning to look back, Alex tugged roughly away from him, taking a step back toward the crowd as he went so that he was between Lorie and the street.

"What?" Lorie whipped toward him, fingers tightening around Alex's wrist, eyes alert and darting for a sign of danger. Alex turned to glare at Lorie, his back to the crowd.

"Let go of me!" Alex snapped.

"What the hell!"

"I said, let go! I'm done with the pair of you dragging me all over this damn city! Honestly, I don't even know why you're still bothering about me since it's not like you have a reason to give a damn."

Lorie's eyes widened.

"Now I said, let go!" Alex yanked, twisting his wrist against Lorie's thumb, pulling out of a grasp that still really had only Raven's inferior strength behind it. As he stumbled backward away from Lorie with more momentum than he'd expected, Alex

IN SHADOWED DREAMS

realized that Lorie must actually have released him a moment before Alex could break his hold.

Then he was stumbling into someone behind him and was turning instinctively to apologize—even in New York falling into a bypasser was considered rude—when he felt someone else slam into his side, knocking him clear of the stranger. Alex twisted, trying to see what was going on behind him, and his eyes widened in the shock of comprehension as he realized what he was seeing. The light of the screens high above them reflected off the sword brooch pinned on the chest of the man whom Alex had just brushed against, and off the bloody knife held in the man's right hand. Between them, and still half pressed against Alex, was Lorie with a red tear in the right shoulder of his sweatshirt.

Alex turned just in time to see Lorie slam his right elbow into the man's nose. The man stumbled backward into the crowd clutching at it, and Alex just had time to see him hit a lady walking past behind him before Lorie's left hand had closed around Alex's wrist again, then Lorie was dragging Alex through the crowd as fast as he could go, no longer making any attempt to look around them or evade their fellow pedestrians.

As they sprinted for the nearest side street, Alex's head was spinning with the attempt to process what had just happened. One of the cultists had found them. He'd been able to get close to them in the crowd, just as Lorie had feared, and Lorie hadn't noticed because Alex had been distracting him. Then, there was that knife. Alex shivered just remembering it. The man had been trying to stab him with it, kill him with it, and he would have done it, too, if Lorie hadn't shoved him out of the way. That was another thing to process. Lorie had saved him, had endangered his own life to protect him. But why?

Before Alex had a chance to ponder that one, however, he felt Lorie stumble ahead of him. Instinctively, Alex reached out, wrapping an arm around Lorie's—Raven's—slighter body, helping to support him as they continued to run. Alex shoved through a wall of pedestrians gawking at the square and ignored the surprised and irritated exclamations all around him, and Lorie dove for a side street. The two pounded down it, their breath rasping in their ears as they ran. Lorie stumbled again, and this time he was so exhausted that Alex's arm wasn't enough to keep him upright. Lorie hit the ground, trying instinctively to break his fall with his hands. He gasped out a curse as a jolt of pain lanced up his injured right arm, and it buckled beneath half his body weight, sending him rolling onto his back, where he lay on the sidewalk, panting and gasping for breath, his knees bleeding from their impact with the concrete.

Alex had also lost his balance as he was pulled downward by the arm still wrapped around Lorie. He let go, stumbling away from Lorie and into the nearby wall of a building. The two of them just stayed like that for a moment, Lorie on the ground and Alex leaning against the wall doubled over, clutching at the stitch in his side, both trying to get their breaths back enough to do anything else. Eventually Lorie sat up, clutching at his head with his left hand and muttering curses under his breath. Alex knelt beside him, peering at the other's bloody arm.

"Is it bad?"

Lorie shook his head. "The arm? No, not deep. Just hurt like a bitch 'cause of how I landed on it, but the knife mostly caught in the sweatshirt. My head though. What the hell is this? I didn't think I hit it when I went down, but it damn well feels like I did."

"I'm guessing that's a migraine. Raven gets them pretty bad. She says stress, exhaustion, and unusual amounts of exercise can trigger them."

"A migraine? Well, fuck! I thought I'd cracked my skull on the sidewalk or something. Any way to get rid of it?"

"Raven keeps some sort of onset meds in her purse, although I don't know exactly which ones or the dose or anything."

Alex glanced around and realized that Raven's purse was nowhere to be seen and that he couldn't remember the last time he'd noticed it, at the movie maybe or on the subway before the whole nightmare began.

"We must have lost it at some point."

Lorie groaned and clutched his head harder and Alex was struck briefly by how upset Raven would be. Never mind her wallet, Raven never went anywhere without her purse or the onset medication it contained. It felt so strange, kneeling in a side street in New York City, completely exhausted and out of breath beside an exhausted and blood-covered Raven who wasn't really Raven, and thinking about how angry the real Raven would be at losing her purse. The mundane nature of the thought only served to amplify the strangeness of his surroundings, and for a moment Alex thought he might lose himself in the disorientation of it all.

"Well, hell! I guess I'm stuck with it then. This is gonna suck."

Lorie's words snapped Alex back to reality, or the semi-fictional whirlpool of bizarre events that seemed to be passing for reality anyway.

"Here," Lorie added, reaching into the pocket of the sweatshirt, pulling out Ari's knife, and held it out to Alex. "Cut the sleeve the rest of the way off. It should be long enough that you can tie it around my shoulder to stop the bleeding.

Alex nodded, eyeing Lorie warily as he took the knife and began trying to figure out how to cut into the sweatshirt without catching Lorie's arm in the process. It was harder than it looked.

"So, why'd you do it? Save me like that, I mean."

"Simple really. It's what Raven brought me here for, after all."

"Raven? But we're not even really friends . . ."

Lorie rolled his eyes. "You really are an idiot, aren't you?"

Alex glared. "What are you—"

"It's like I said," Lorie interrupted, talking over him. "Magic was going down, and she realized that without it you lot would all be defenseless. And it's not like she was in much physical shape to look after herself, let alone you guys. I don't have access to all of her thoughts and memories, just basic stuff like who she was and who you guys are and where I come from, and her immediate thoughts from right before she summoned me."

Alex flinched at the use of the word "was" to describe Raven. He did not like the way that sounded, like she was never coming back. No matter how much he had been starting to hate her, the thought of her permanently replaced by this fictional assassin was not a pleasant one.

"From what I can get from her memories, she figured that she had only a few minutes to cast something that'd protect you all, but it had to be something that wouldn't need magic to maintain it, something for keeps that wouldn't be affected by the barrier. So she decided to try summoning someone into her body who could make better use of it, since she figured that once the summoning was done, magic wouldn't be needed to maintain it. I was the most logical choice. She'd been rereading my books ever since Book 5 came out, so I was fresh in her head, which meant that she was more likely to be able to pull it off, and I don't use magic or anything like that, so I wouldn't be affected by the barrier. Plus, my third book is set in New York, so I know the place, which made aligning herself with me easier. That was some of why it worked. But I don't think it would have if her mindset and mine hadn't aligned so well."

Alex frowned. There was something that had been bothering him for a while. "You're awfully calm about being a fictional character."

Lorie shrugged his uninjured shoulder. "Guess so. It's part of the knowledge that I picked up when I was dropped in here. Guess it's kind of weird to think about, but it wasn't weird to Raven, and I'm still looking at this world through her eyes and memories, so . . ." He shrugged again.

Alex shook his head. If someone tried to tell him that he was fiction, that neither he nor anyone he cared about was real, that he and every bad thing that had ever happened to him had just been invented to fulfill the whims of some author, he wouldn't be anywhere near as calm, but if Lorie was coping with it, far be it from him to upset the man.

"So she summoned you to protect her body?"

"Haven't you been listening?" Lorie snapped. "Raven's gone! Maybe for good! Does that sound like I'm just protecting her body?"

"I . . ."

Lorie yanked his injured arm out of Alex's hand, spinning to face Alex full on, and in the same movement, bringing himself into a kneeling position so that their eyes were more or less on a level. Alex instinctively flinched away from the look in Lorie's eyes. For the first time since they'd met, the hitman looked really angry. It only lasted for a moment though, because the next thing he knew Lorie was doubled over swearing and clutching his head with his good arm.

"You ok?"

"Moved too fast! Stupid head! Just when I thought it was dying down!"

"Ah . . ." Whenever she was symptomatic, Alex had noticed that Raven always became incredibly carful in her movements. It was one of her tells, one he'd eventually learned to notice and interpret even before she told him that she was currently symptomatic. But then, Lorie had himself said that he didn't have all of Raven's memories.

Lorie leaned against the wall, breathing hard and glaring up at Alex.

"It was the three of you, idiot! It was all about protecting the three of you!"

"Are you su—"

"Do you know," Lorie asked, talking over Alex, "where Raven was going when she ran off?"

"Um, Central Park?" Alex ventured.

"Central Park. More specifically, the boat pond. And do you know why?"

Alex shook his head.

"She knew the more closely she could align her mindset with mine, the more likely she'd be able to pull off summoning me. Do you know what she was going to do when she got there?"

Alex shook his head again.

"There was a scene during my time in New York when I got double-crossed and ended up getting ambushed in Central Park. I was out on one of the row boats and there was a fight. Anyway, I ended up getting pushed in, only I can't really swim, so I was half drowned before Xander managed to fish me out. If Raven couldn't summon me on the way there and she got to the pond before the barrier went up, she was going to throw herself in and half drown herself, hoping it would work!"

Alex stared. "What?"

But Lorie wasn't done.

"You know why I suggested we separate from the others? Raven knew that you were more awake than either of them, so you'd be more of a target, and she was more awake than any of you, so she'd be even more of one. She thought about ditching you guys to keep you safe, only she thought that even if the other two didn't attract attention, you probably would, and you wouldn't stand a chance on your own. Without us the two of them should make it back fine; this close to the station they're in a lot less danger without us. But she knew she couldn't protect you."

"So . . . so, wait . . ." Alex shook his head trying to process. "Wait. Are you saying that Raven let you take over her body just so she could . . . but . . . that's . . . I thought she didn't care about me . . ."

"Didn't care about you!" Lorie actually laughed a little at that.

"Well, she said—"

"Like I said," Lorie talked over him again. "I honestly don't think it would have worked if Raven's mindset hadn't lined up with mine so well. I have this, well I guess I might even call him a close friend these days, though I'd never tell him that. He's, Xander's, an investigative journalist. Our paths kept crossing and, at first, he was always making problems for me, making my job harder by trying to get stories on some of my targets and getting close to them in ways that made them harder to get. But then this asshole businessman client of mine double-crossed me in London and . . . well, anyway, the point is a smart journalist can end up coming in handy sometimes.

"We ran into each other every now and then after that, and he started asking me to let him write a profile piece on me. Like hell I was going to do that. I like my job. I kept telling him that you can't be a hitman if everyone knows all about you or if your employers think that you're going to spill all their secrets to the press and that I really just wasn't that invested in him getting a Pulitzer. Eventually I guess I started looking out for him. See, there's some stuff about him that some people really don't like and, honestly, I worry about him a lot these days. Sometimes it's more than that; sometimes I'm really scared for him, and that feeling"—Lorie's voice had softened a little as he talked about his friend, but then it sharpened again—"that feeling that I feel about Xander is what Raven was feeling about you!"

Alex stared at Lorie, his thoughts racing. Part of his brain was absently running through what he remembered of what Raven had told him about Lorie and his story. He remembered her mentioning Xander. He had been one of Raven's favorite characters: clever, quick witted, and always ready to get himself into a sticky situation in order to provoke an incriminating comment to catch on his tape recorder. Mostly though, Alex was simply trying to wrap his head around Lorie's words. The Raven that Lorie was describing sounded far more like the Raven Alex had thought he'd known than the Raven he had seen that night. Raven cared. He'd known that. He'd always known that.

He cared and Raven cared, but . . .

"Xander."

"Huh?"

"Your friend. His name's Xander, right? Like the other half of mine. You said that in order to summon you, Raven needed to align her mind with yours, so could she have—"

"Weren't you listening?" Alex recoiled, as much from the anger in Lorie's eyes as from his shout. "You can't fake emotions like that! You can't just pretend! The whole point is that they have to be real or it doesn't fucking work!"

Alex looked at the ground, the last of his anger at Raven melting away. If he was being honest with himself, he'd already let most of it go before he'd asked Lorie about the names. It didn't make sense. He'd known that. Lorie really was able to read some of Raven's thoughts and memories—the fact that he had even known their names proved that much. And you couldn't fake emotion like that, not from the inside anyway. Still, he'd had to ask. It had been one last, pathetic attempt to hold onto his anger. Anger, which Raven had always referred to as the best defense. Anger, which was the only thing keeping the fear at bay. Anger, which meant that he didn't have to confront what a complete idiot he'd been. Well, he had to confront it now.

Alex realized that he was still kneeling on the sidewalk, one fist clenched against the pavement and that his vision had blurred. He was crying. He was crying because he'd been such an idiot, but it was more than that; he was crying because letting go of his anger at Raven meant that he was forced to think about what Lorie had said about her, everything that Lorie had said about her. *"This body's mine now." "Raven's gone! Maybe for good!"*

"Undo it." Alex's voice was soft.

"Huh?"

"Undo it. Please. I . . . I need to talk to her."

"I told you, no can't do."

"I know she wanted you to look out for us, but still, I told you: Undo it."

Lorie had to listen. He had to undo it. Raven. Alex needed to see a her that was actually her, to talk to her, to tell her he was sorry for being such a jerk.

"And I told you, I can't." Lorie was starting to sound irritated again, but this time he wasn't the only one.

"Why not? Is it because you're a hitman? You think you should get paid first for keeping us alive?"

"I take it all back. You're nothing like Xander. *He* would have listened to what I'm actually saying and not whatever it is you think you're hearing!"

"I . . ."

"I didn't say I *won't* undo it. I said I *can't!* Get that through your thick skull. It's not about me wanting to; I literally can't!"

Alex sat back on his heels, staring at Lorie. The irritation on his face, the way he'd turned his head away in exasperation; it was so, so normal. It made his chest hurt. Maybe it was the fact that Lorie had inherited some of Raven's memories, or maybe it was simply a shared quirk of body language. Hell, maybe, knowing Raven, she'd read a description of Lorie's body language in one of his books and deliberately mimicked the posture. Whatever the case, the expression was so, so Raven that Alex found it all but impossible to believe that the person sitting in front of him could be anyone other than his friend.

"Why not?" he asked softly, tearing his eyes again from the painfully familiar sight before him.

"Because I don't know a damn thing about magic."

"Huh? But everything you said . . ."

"Everything I told you was just what was rattling around in Raven's head, stuff she was thinking about that I was able to pick up on. But magic itself," Lorie let out an exasperated huff. He sounded genuinely annoyed. "I don't know how the hell that's supposed to work and just dropping me into some fantasy world didn't change that."

"Fantasy world? This isn't—"

"Isn't it? Mages running through the streets of New York? Ancient magic-stealing cults? People who have the ability to capture my world as a book and other people who can summon me out of it just by bleeding and thinking some stuff? Magic's not real. It's just a fairy story for kids and people who don't know how science works, yet here I am in the body of some college kid. What else do you call this besides a fantasy world?"

"Oh." Alex said it softly as Lorie's words sank in. It made sense. *Shadows of the Silver Towers* was a series of crime drama novels. At least, as far as Alex knew, they weren't fantastic at all. Of course, Lorie didn't believe in magic. Of course, he thought it was just fiction. A few hours ago, Alex would have said the same. Thought about like that, it made sense that Lorie would see this as the fantasy world. It explained, perhaps, some of the calm that had seemed so strange to Alex. If Lorie saw this all as unreality, as a novel come to life and nothing more . . . The irony of the thought wasn't lost on Alex, but it also didn't distract him from the magnitude of the problem.

Raven had used magic to summon Lorie before the barrier went up, so, presumably, magic would be needed to undo it. The barrier was still in place, but even if it wasn't or they got outside of it, that didn't change the fact that magic would be needed to undo whatever it was that Raven had done. Raven said that he had magic. He had even felt it, the heat running through his blood, warning him of danger. Yet he didn't know the first thing about using it. He didn't even know if, when not directly reacting to another mage, he *could* use it. He certainly didn't have the first clue how to go about undoing whatever the hell it was that Raven had done. The only thing he did know was that whatever Raven had done, she had done from the inside, acting on her own mind and body in a way that had to do with the state of her mind's internal landscape, with little reference to the external one. That meant, presumably, that if there was a way to undo whatever it was that it must also be internal, and there was the problem. Raven wasn't the one on the inside anymore. Lorie was. Even if Raven had known how to undo it, she hadn't been thinking about it, so Lorie didn't know what to do, and the only real clue they had was that it would mean using magic, something Lorie couldn't do.

Alex reeled, pressing an arm against the wall to steady himself as the reality of the situation washed over him. He had no earthly idea what to do, and there was no one he could ask. This nightmare had swallowed Raven, and he didn't have the first idea how to get her back. Ever. All he knew was that one moment she'd been there and the next she hadn't. Now there was some strange fictional being wearing Raven's skin like a coat. And Raven was, Raven was . . . He refused to think the word "gone." Instead, he searched desperately for another word and, in his struggle, he realized what he hadn't asked.

"Where is she?"

"Huh?" Lorie looked slightly confused.

"Where is she?" Alex asked again. "If you're in her body, then where is Raven?"

Lorie blinked, looking almost taken aback by the question. "I . . ." He paused, frowning, his voice unsure. "I don't know." He said it slowly. Then, gently. "She might not be anywhere."

"What?" Alex half choked on the word.

Lorie shook his head sadly. "It's possible. When she summoned me, she overwrote my mind and memories onto hers. It's possible that doing so was permanent, that it was like saving over a computer file, erasing the old saved file in the process of updating it."

Alex stared at him in horror.

Lorie shivered. "Hell, if that were the case, I might not even be Lawrence Rain at all. If I'm right about that then I might actually *be* Raven, just with my—that is, Lorie's—memories, plastered on top." Lorie shook his head again, looking highly frustrated. "I really don't like that idea."

"Nor I . . ." Alex's voice caught and cracked with emotion. He cleared his throat and tried again. "I don't like it either." Just trying to wrap his head around the implications and the implicit questions about whether or not it is the memories that make the self was enough to give Alex a headache, and he wasn't the one with the chronic migraines. And maybe focusing on that would be enough to distract him from the part where his friend was essentially dead.

"That's not the only possibility though," Lorie said, shooting Alex a surprisingly sympathetic look. He tapped his forehead. "She could also still be here somewhere."

Lorie began unsteadily climbing to his feet, using the wall as support. He grimaced once when he straightened his injured knees and again when he turned his head to look back down at Alex.

"We've stayed still for way too long. We can keep talking as we go, but we need to move."

He tried to take one step away from the wall, winced, and clutched at his head.

"Damn it! Does this pain ever stop? It wasn't this bad a minute ago!"

"They're positional." Alex stood automatically. "Raven always says that they get worse the more vertical she is."

"Fucking perfect! What fucking wonderful luck!" He started walking, clutching at his head with one hand as he went, the other resting, seemingly automatically, on the bulge of the waistband and sweatshirt that Alex knew still concealed the gun.

Privately, Alex thought of telling Lorie that he *was* lucky. When Raven's migraines got really bad, she couldn't even stand or carry on a conversation, let alone do both, but he thought better of it. It wasn't like it would help any. Pain was pain, and being told that it's "not as bad as" had never helped anyone. Ever.

Alex hurried after Lorie. When he came up beside the other man, the mercenary turned to him, eyes serious.

"It's true. Raven might be gone, but I don't think she is. I don't have any proof, just a feeling, but I think Raven might still be in here somewhere."

Alex nodded, eyes flickering away, unsure what to say, only knowing that every fiber of his being was hoping that Lorie's feeling was right.

"We talked a bit on the way back to the station. It helped keep Lorie's mind off of the migraine and mine off of, well, everything. Lorie told me as much as he could get from Raven's memories about magic and how it worked and what he could figure out about hers. We were pretty close to Grand Central at that point, and we stuck to the shadows. No one paid any attention to us. When we were about halfway between Times Square and the train station, my phone started ringing. It was Ari. Turns out she'd been texting me the whole time, but I'd had my phone on vibrate, a holdover from the movie, so I hadn't noticed. She was mad that I hadn't responded. I guess I'd really freaked her out. She said that they'd made it back to the station and were actually on the train, although it wasn't leaving for another 15 minutes. I told her I'd be there soon. I just trying to figure out what I was going to tell them about Raven . . ." Alex's voice trailed away and he shook his head.

"So what did you?" Liza prompted.

"Did I?"

"Tell them."

"Oh that." Alex smiled a little. "I didn't. I hung up on her before she could ask."

Alex ran a hand ruefully through his hair. "I knew she'd be mad at me for that later, but I still hadn't even figured out how to put it all into words for myself, let alone anyone else. I figured that that way I'd have till we got to the train to figure out how to explain it all. I was right, in a way, but it wasn't quite the explanation I'd been planning to give."

They had finally reached the station. A wave of relief washed over Alex as he saw the familiar doors ahead of him, but Lorie pulled him back. Alex turned to look at him, surprised. Lorie was a little more than a silhouette standing where the gray of a New York City night met the actual darkness of the shadow cast by a nearby building, and Alex was reminded abruptly of the name of the series from which the hitman came: *Shadows of the Silver Towers.* He was starting to understand it.

"What?"

"I just figured I should say goodbye."

Alex blinked. "You're not coming?" It had never occurred to him.

Lorie snorted in slight amusement. "Have you seen me?"

"Huh?"

As if to highlight his point, a cab sped by a bit too close to the curb, bathing them both briefly in the yellow glow of its headlights. Alex sucked in his breath. He saw what Lorie meant, for if he had thought Lorie looked like a horror movie after killing the gunman, it was nothing to how he looked now. Raven's hair, dyed black and streaked with silver, the red of her sweatshirt, and the paleness of her skin created a backdrop that might as well have been chosen specifically to emphasize the blood, and there was a lot of blood. Blood and newly forming scabs covered Lorie's knees from when he had scraped them falling. Lorie's left arm still bore lines of now dry blood from where Raven had cut herself to summon him, and his right hand was also still covered in the blood of the man whose arm he'd slashed. Topping the image off was Lorie's right sleeve, which Alex had roughly hacked off and tied around his upper right arm to stop yet more bleeding. It had mostly done the job but not before blood had time to coat a large amount of the uncovered part of Lorie's upper arm as well. And then, of course, there was the suspicious-looking gun bulge at Lorie's hip.

"Oh."

"Yeah, oh." Lorie still sounded rather amused. "It's dark enough out here that between that and the fact that New Yorkers make a practice of not paying attention to anyone they don't know, no one's noticed or called the police, but in there? Security would be all over me."

"Hmm. Maybe if you rolled down the one sleeve and put your hands in your pockets, or—"

Lorie shook his head, cutting Alex off, his expression turning serious.

"Even if I wasn't covered in blood, I still wouldn't be coming with you."

"What? Why not?"

"I'm not Raven."

"Yeah, I know. But still, it's not like you have anywhere else to go . . .."

Lorie gave him a small smile. "Thanks. But still. If I went back with you, I'd have to pretend to be Raven, and you'd have to play along. It wouldn't be fair to anyone. You'd be in mourning for your friend, but you'd still have to pretend I was her, and you'd have to help me pretend, and in the end you'd hate me for it. There's no way I'd pretend perfectly, so her other friends would notice some change, but they wouldn't know what, and in the end the memory of the-her-that-was-me would overwrite their memory of her. And of course, I'd have to pretend that I'm someone I'm not, which wouldn't be fun for me either."

Alex nodded slowly. He felt like he should argue but Lorie was right on all three counts, and he knew it. Still . . .

"Will you be ok, though?"

Lorie smiled again, amused this time. "Don't worry about me. I'm a professional. I can take care of myself."

"But this isn't your world."

"True. But even if the people aren't the same, the city itself is. I know how things work in cities like this one. I'll be fine."

Alex nodded again, looking away. Maybe it was just that Lorie was occupying a body that Alex was used to feeling protective toward, but he still felt like he ought not to leave him behind, alone in the city without any money, or place to go, and with people still trying to kill him. And yet . . .

"You should go."

Alex's eyes snapped back to Lorie.

"If you keep standing here, you run the risk of getting attacked again, and your train leaves in 6 minutes. Text me once you're on the train so that I know you've gotten clear of the city. I'll hold onto Raven's phone, so if you need me you'll be able to reach me. And don't worry about her; I'll take care of her."

Alex nodded slowly. He tried to say something, but the words wouldn't form. He tried again.

"Thank you."

Lorie blinked and a fleeting look of surprise crossed his face. Then he nodded back, and Alex turned toward the crosswalk. He headed for the train station and the train that would take him far away from this waking nightmare. There was nothing more to say. He looked back once though, just before passing out of the gloom of the city night and into the brightness of the well-lit station beyond the large double doors. Lorie had gone, disappeared back into that gloom. One more shadow going who knows where within that sea of silver towers. Yes, Alex understood the name, but whether he understood the man? That was another question entirely.

When Alex finished, they both sat in silence for a while. Alex was looking down at his phone again, presumably lost in memory. Liza was still taking it all in. Alex's story was incredible, absolutely incredible. For most of her life, she had known magic was real, ever since that trip to Cornwall when she was eight, but still . . . "Still nothing," she told herself. She had already known about New York. She had already known that it wasn't the first incursion and that it wouldn't be the last. Sure enough, here they were again. She knew very few awake mages. They were hard to find—really, it was just a matter of luck—which was why she'd been lucky to find Alex and why they needed all the help they could get. It was why she needed to stop marveling over Alex's story and start giving some serious thought to his proposal.

Alex had mentioned Lorie when she had said they needed allies. That meant what? Using Lorie to take out the cultists before they could set up their perimeter? The thought made her want to vomit. The idea of hiring someone to go and kill people, just like that, was one that she had even more trouble coming to terms with than the wildest story that Alex could tell. And yet . . . and yet, she was the one who had decided to put a stop to this incursion. She had known that simply allowing it to occur would mean that people would be killed, people like her, killed for the crime of being like her. She couldn't allow it, not when she was in a position to stop it. She knew that stopping it would mean fighting, and if she was going to fight, it had to be to win. That meant that she couldn't discard an option just because she didn't find it palatable. The simple fact was—and her stomach churned just thinking it—that, no matter what happened, people were going to die. The only question that remained for her to answer was whether they would be the innocent sleepers or the cultists who had started the whole thing, and she already knew which she would prefer.

"Alex."

He looked up.

"Can you contact him?"

PART 2

THE WAKING SLEEP

Lorie had to catch himself before he slammed into the hotel and demanded to know where Xander was. He forced himself to slow to a walk, to relax his shoulders, to drop his cell phone back into his pocket. He even plastered a slightly abashed smile on his face. As he pushed open the door, he made sure his gait was light and unhurried, more casual tourist then angry assassin.

There was one person ahead of him at the reception desk and Lorie balled his hands into fists in his pockets in frustration as he waited in simulated patience for the man to finish chatting up the receptionist and go about his business. The man was tall and dark-haired and looked to be in his forties. His suit and body language said traveling businessman, but Lorie made a point of watching him carefully, just in case. He didn't stare. Staring would have been worse than not watching at all. Instead, Lorie let his eyes wander across the man and around the lobby, taking in the location of steps, elevator, and back entrance, before returning them to the man who was finally moving away from the reception desk.

Lorie moved to stand in front of it as quickly as he dared. Once there, he smiled sheepishly down at the receptionist and rubbed at the back of his neck in what he knew would appear an obvious display of awkwardness.

"Yes? What can I do for you?" the receptionist asked, returning his smile with one that looked as though it had been painted on by someone who hadn't bothered waiting for the basecoat to dry all the way. When she had spoken, her words had been in clipped, accentless Russian, and Lorie could easily have responded in the same, but he did not. Instead, he adopted a brokenly stumbling speech pattern and heavy American accent which made clear exactly how little time he had spent on this side of the Atlantic.

"Um, excuse me, ma'am. I'm looking for my brother. He's traveling for work just now and it's his birthday and I happened to be in Europe on business myself, so I figured I'd take the day to hop over and surprise him, only"—and here he gave the receptionist another one of his sheepish smiles—"I don't actually know what his room number is, and it's not like I can ask him without giving the game away, so . . ." He trailed off, looking hopefully down at her.

"I see. And what is your brother's name, please?"

"It's Xander, Xander Myers."

She nodded and typed something onto her keyboard. "Here he is, room 204." She reached for the phone automatically.

(And now for the hard part.)

"Actually"—he raised one hand to forestall her—"would you mind not calling up to him? It's only I've come all this way to surprise him, so I'd like it to be a full-on surprise, if you catch my meaning . . ." He let his voice trail away, smiling hopefully at her again.

Either she'd entirely bought the act or she decided that whatever Lorie really wanted was well above her paygrade because she nodded agreeably and gestured him toward the elevator. With another smile and a wave of thanks, Lorie turned and walked briskly off in the direction she indicated. (Elevator or stairs?) If she changed her mind once he got out of sight and decided to warn

Xander anyway, which one would the reporter choose to take? The steps probably, Lorie decided and directed his feet accordingly.

As soon as the door to the stairwell closed behind him, Lorie dropped all pretense and bolted up the steps, taking them two at a time. Reaching the landing, he raced down the second-floor hallway and pounded on door 204 until he heard the sound of the chain being undone. When the door finally swung open, it did so to reveal a man who appeared to be in his early- to mid-twenties, short and slender with close-cropped red-brown hair and clever hazel eyes. The man was dressed in short black combat boots, dark jeans, and a white button-down, the sleeves of which were rolled up and the neck of which was buttoned up to the man's throat.

"Lori, what a pleasant surprise!" Xander smiled mockingly up at him, an expression that did not do anything to temper the serious look in the younger man's eyes.

"Save it!" Lorie snapped. "You know exactly why I'm here! Now are we going to do this where the whole hallway can hear me or are you going to let me in?"

Rather than give Xander a chance to ponder that one, Lorie immediately followed his words up by stepping forward and pushing his way into the room beyond. Apparently deciding that he might as well give way to the inevitable, Xander made no move to bar Lori's intrusion and allowed the door to slam shut behind his uninvited guest.

"Now," Lorie all but snarled, glaring down at Xander, "what the hell sort of mess do you think you're getting yourself into?"

"I'm following the story." Xander's words were calm and his face had turned impassive.

"If you go through with this, you're going to end up dead, and you know it!"

"You make it sound like this is the first time I've done something like this, and you know it's not."

"And what happens if they figure out what you are?" Lorie snapped.

"What I am?" There was a hint of danger in Xander's tone. "/What/?"

"You know what I mean!"

"Come on, I'm not that bad of a liar. There's no reason they should guess I'm a journalist."

"That's not what I'm talking about, and you know it!" Lorie was angry enough that for once he wasn't being cautious.

"So is this because I'm trans or because I'm Jewish then?" Suddenly the casual tone was gone from Xander's voice, and there was real anger in his eyes.

"Xander, these people, they don't like people like you . . ."

"No one does." The journalist's voice was still calm, but Lorie could hear the anger, and yes bitterness, in his words.

"You're not listening to me!" Lorie dug his nails into his palms in an attempt to keep from grabbing the younger man by the shoulders and shaking him until he started paying attention. "This isn't like back home; it isn't safe for you here!"

"If by home you mean the US, it's not safe for a person like me there either. You're from Pittsburgh, Lorie, you should know that better than most."

Lorie froze, all of the angry energy draining out of him with that single name. "How do you know"—his voice had dropped back to a more normal volume, and it was shaking slightly—"that I'm from Pittsburgh."

Xander smiled up at him, an expression that held just a touch of amusement and remarkably little warmth. "I have my sources, and I told you I'd be doing my research."

"I didn't expect you to find anything though . . ."

Both the amusement and the warmth grew in Xander's face in response to the other man's honesty.

"Really, Lorie, you should know me better by now. Don't invite me to dig if you don't want me finding things. Yes, I know you're from Pittsburgh; I know you picked that particular city because you wanted someplace big enough to disappear into but, ironic as it seems now, small and peaceful enough that you wouldn't have to worry about working in your own backyard. Just like I know that you're a lot less worried about me finding out where you're from than you are about what will happen to your sister and niece if anyone finds out that you bought them a house in Squirrel Hill. Well, don't. You know your secret is safe with me, and my sources aren't ones that others would be able to use."

With that, Xander pushed lightly past Lorie, who made no move to stop him, and pulled open the hotel room door. Halfway through it, Xander turned to glance back at him.

"Thanks for the concern; I mean it. There's a thumb drive on the nightstand for you. Look through it, then do me a favor and make sure it disappears." Then the door was swinging shut behind him, and Lorie was left staring at the closed door and wondering what the hell had just happened.

—From Book 2 of *Shadows of the Silver Towers* by A. B. Levinson

(NOW)

New Jersey was gray and rainy, and Alex wondered if that was part of why the bar looked so seedy. No, he decided, the bar was just really seedy. He wasn't sure exactly where they were—Liza had been driving—and he didn't know New Jersey particularly well anyway, but he could tell that they weren't exactly in the nicest of neighborhoods. Still, this was where they'd been told to come, so . . . He looked around the room. Some people sat in high-backed booths, others talked at small round tables and over at the bar. A head turned, black hair streaked with silver, and two, slightly unnerving, black eyes fixed on him and Liza.

Alex froze. He couldn't help it. It had been months, months since he'd seen Raven, months in which a day had never gone by when he didn't think about her, months that made it almost impossible not to run to her now, made it almost impossible to remember that this, this wasn't Raven.

He took a shaky breath as Lorie stood, leaving the bar and waving them over to an empty booth. No one else paid them any attention. As he walked toward the booth, Alex was able to get his first good look at Lorie. What Alex saw surprised him. Lorie wore hiking boots, black jeans, and an overlarge white T-shirt with a faded National Parks logo on the front. The loose cut of the shirt made the body he wore look younger than Alex knew it to be, but that wasn't what surprised him. Until that moment, Alex hadn't really thought about it, but as soon he saw Lorie, it struck him how strange it was that Raven's body should still look like, well, Raven.

"Your hair." It was the first thing he said when Lorie reached them.

"Huh?"

Alex sucked in a breath. As Lorie spoke, he turned toward Alex, revealing an additional change—a thin scar running longwise down Raven's right cheek.

"What happened?"

"Oh, that." Lorie touched two fingers to the scar, then gestured at the booth with his other hand. "Here. Sit, sit."

They slid into the booth, and Liza eyed Lorie curiously as he slid into the seat across from them. After everything that Alex had said, she couldn't help but wonder about the *being* that sat in front of her.

"It's from a fight I got into in a bar, a couple days after I got here. Some guys took a bit more of an interest in me than I'm used to, and I ended up having to teach them all a lesson about where not to put their hands. But it was before I'd gotten used to having long hair and one of them grabbed it, which made dodging a bit harder." He shrugged. "It wasn't as deep as they would have liked, and I paid them back for it, but after that I learned how to braid my hair so that it stays out of my way. Like this it's easy enough to stuff down the back of my shirt when a fight starts."

"But why'd you leave it long? I mean why not just cut it off?"

"Oh, that's what you meant." Lorie rolled the end of his braid back and forth absently between his fingers.

"This isn't my body. It's Raven's. I didn't figure it was my place to go changing it."

Alex blinked. "Is that why you've even re-dyed her hair?"

Lorie nodded. "Figured that's how she liked it."

Then he shook his head. "Damn, but it's been harder than I thought. My hair's long enough to tie back, so I figured I knew what long hair was like, but all the dyeing and the streaking, and figuring out how to do a tight French braid—I had no idea. The number of hours of tutorials I had to watch . . ."

Lorie trailed off as Liza snorted with laughter at his obvious dismay. Alex, however, did not laugh; he was too busy staring thoughtfully at Lorie.

"You still sound like you're just guarding her body."

Lorie nodded slowly, the amusement leaving his eyes, and Liza thought that he looked tired.

"I hope so."

"You do?" Liza asked, curious.

Lorie just looked at her coolly.

"Oh right, Liza, this is Lorie. Lorie, Liza. I told her everything."

Lorie gave Liza a nod of greeting.

"Yeah, I do. I miss the people from my world. My sister and my niece. And Xander too, I guess, or at least I worry about them. I know it's not logical to worry, since it's not like anything can happen while I'm gone, but I'd still rather not be here by the time the next book comes out. Whatever's coming for me, reading about it instead of living it . . ." He shook his head.

Alex started trying to figure out how that would work, and if Lorie really would be able to return to his story or if this version of Lorie would simply wink out of existence if he were ever displaced. Before he could think about it for too long, however, he was interrupted by the sound of Lorie clearing his throat.

"But that's not why you wanted to see me after all this time. I know a client meeting when I see one. So, what is it that you want to hire me to do?"

Liza blinked, refocusing her eyes, and with them, her mind. She had been staring thoughtfully at Lorie, an idea niggling at her mind. Later, she decided. She'd bring it up later, after she'd explained what they'd come here for.

"You're right about me. I am looking to hire you."

"Oh really?" Lorie's eye's narrowed and a small smile traced his lips. "And who are you looking to kill?"

"I don't, I mean, that is . . ." Liza choked on her response. She supposed it was true enough. That was what she was here for, to hire him to kill. But hearing it spoken of so calmly when she was still struggling to come to terms with it herself . . . That was more than she could handle. Before she could figure out how to formulate a coherent response, however, Alex cut across her spluttering.

"They're coming back."

Lorie's eyes, which had been fixed on Liza with a mixture of amusement and derision, snapped to Alex.

"Back?"

Alex nodded.

"Liza is mage-born too. She's the one who found out."

Lorie's eyes returned to Liza, with considerably more interest this time.

"I awakened as a result of a vacation my parents and I took to Cornwall when I was eight. While we were staying in the town of Boscastle, I made friends with a local kid named Maya. She and I went exploring one day, and we stumbled across something we shouldn't have, a group of cultists. Well, it's a long story and not particularly relevant, but suffice it to say that it turned out we were both sleepers, and we awakened as a result. After everything that summer, we kept in touch. She's been keeping an eye on some of the cult activity up there, and three days ago she tipped me off that they were planning to fly into Newark Airport and look for an area with a lot of mages to target. That's when I started looking for other awake mages to help me deal with them, only it's not like there's an address book I can search or anything, so the best I could do was get the other two awake mages I know at my school to help me look for more. Grace, Charlotte, and I figured that the best chance we had was to split up and travel to as many different colleges as we could and just sort of wander around their campuses in hopes of sensing someone."

"Why?" Lorie sounded genuinely confused.

"We needed to narrow the search down somehow and we've noticed that they tend to have a higher population of mage-born then most other places. Schools in general do, I mean, not just colleges since you end up with people from all different backgrounds in a way you wouldn't at any one business or office. It's not like we want to go getting kids involved if we can help it though, which is why we've been limiting our search to colleges. The vast majority are sleepers, of course, but we figured there had to be at least a few who weren't."

"Your school, so you're a teacher then?"

"A student."

"You're in college? You don't look like it."

Liza nodded, not seaming particularly bothered by what Alex thought had been a rather rude question. "I am, and I don't because I'm twenty-eight. I was having, well, let's just say some issues with magic around the time most people normally go to college, so I'm only now getting my Associates."

"Ah. So you and your friends split up and wandered from campus to campus and that's how you found Alex?"

Liza nodded. "Exactly. Grace wanted to try to wake some of the sleepers, but I said no because as long as they're asleep, they're much less likely to be in danger. But if we woke them up right now, it'd be like painting a target on their backs."

"So instead, Alex suggested that you come to me." That small, almost mocking, smile was back. "Very well. I can help you. Tell me when your cultists are arriving, and I'll make sure that they don't bother anyone. No need for any of your people to be involved."

"Really?"

Lorie nodded. "It'll be easier that way. I'll need all the information your informant friend can get on them though, and before that, let's talk about my fee."

"Fee?" Alex stared.

"Well, yeah. I'm a hitman, after all. This is my job. If you want my help, you'll have to hire me."

"But last time—"

"Last time Raven hired me."

"Lorie—"

"It's ok, Alex." Liza's voice cut calmly across the other two. She rubbed thoughtfully at the side of her face. "I think I know what I can offer."

"Oh?"

"Earlier, when you said you wanted to give that body back to Raven, did you mean it?"

The mocking smile vanished from Lorie's lips, and his eyes turned serious.

"I did."

Alex twisted to stare wide-eyed at Liza.

"Wait! You can do that?"

Liza tilted her head to one side, as though trying to figure out how to phrase her next response. At last she said, "In a manner of speaking, I might know a way."

"What do you mean 'in a manner of speaking'?"

"I mean that I can't but I think . . . I think there's a chance you can."

"Me?"

Liza nodded.

"From everything you've said, I'm guessing you have the right of it. What Raven did, if it's undoable at all—and I can't be sure that it is—but if it is, it probably does have to be undone from the inside."

"So then how . . . ?"

"My guess is, if Lorie's right and she still lives, then she's inside there somewhere, locked in her own inner world, unable or unwilling to reclaim her body. If that's the case, then the only thing that I can think of which might have a chance of changing that is for someone to go in and get her."

"Go and get her?"

"Right. Enter her inner landscape, her inner world. I'm guessing that her mind would try to reject most such visitors as intrusions, but you, as her friend, I think you might well be able to do so."

Alex frowned. "Ok, but how? I can't just, just snap my fingers and be inside of someone's mind."

"That's where I come in. I, too, am a mage and, unlike you, have been awake for almost my entire life. Magic cleaves to magic, and Raven's internal landscape has already been altered by a spell once. My magic works mostly off instinct, so I can't predict what you'll experience, and I don't have any idea how I'd go about pulling you out again, so you or Raven will have to figure that out, but I'm pretty sure I can get you inside. It is risky though. You could get stuck."

Alex looked taken aback for a moment, and for just a breath Liza thought she spotted a touch of fear in his eyes. Then one of Alex's hands closed around his cell phone again and he shook his head.

"I figured there'd be some risk. Still though! We have to try. I owe her at least that!" Alex's eyes burned with sudden fire. "That is . . ." The determination in his voice suddenly faltered, and he turned to Lorie.

Liza realized that Lorie had not spoken since she had made her offer. He simply watched them with an unreadable expression, as though lost in thought.

"Lorie, I—" Alex began but Lorie cut him off with a nod.

"I accept."

"You do?" Liza asked, slightly surprised, despite the fact that she herself was the one who had had made the offer. She, too, had realized that leaving Raven's body might be the end of Lorie's existence.

"Yes. I'm tired, tired of living in a world without my friends and family, and I inherited enough of Raven's memories to care about what happens to her. I'll accept this job and your promise of payment, and once I complete the job, I will expect you to do everything you can to uphold your end of your bargain."

PART 3

IN SHADOWED DREAMS

Dammit! The thought was an oddly detached one as Lorie felt the cold water wrap around him. He struggled, his arms flailing, his feet kicking wildly, his neck craned upward, straining to keep his head above the water. He made a grab for the side of the rowboat, but it was already far beyond his reach. Rising just above his splashing and the desperate pounding of his heart, Lorie could hear laughter drifting back to him through the night air as it pulled farther away, leaving him behind.

In any other circumstance Lorie would have been cursing, but at the moment all of his breath was being absorbed into the singular effort that was his attempt to keep his mouth and nose above the surface of the boat pond. As for what he was going to do after that, he had not a clue. He had watched swimming on TV before, he had even taken his niece to the pool over the summer and paddled with her in three-foot-deep water, but this was scarcely closer to that experience than the television had been. Lori's arms were getting tired. Physically he was in shape, athletic even, but the differences between using his muscles for running or self-defense training and using them for something with which he had no experience, coupled with his wild flailing, were burning him out faster than he would have thought possible.

Lorie's head sunk beneath the water. Driven by a surge of increasing desperation, he managed to push it back up into the air again, taking one long desperate breath before he sank once more. The world was growing gray and fuzzy around the edges, and he knew with an oddly detached part of his brain that he was probably drowning. Again, he managed to force his head above the water and again he sank back into the murky depths. His feet kicked wildly, trying to propel him upward, but his arms were too tired to be of much assistance anymore. Dimly even as he struggled, he recognized that it might already be too late. What an utterly ridiculous way to die! Lawrence Rain, infamous hitman known the world over, found drowned in the Manhattan boat pond.

Just then, Lorie felt a pressure around his chest and side, different somehow from the bands that felt like they were wrapping themselves around his lungs. He was pulled sideways and upward and, as he kicked out again, Lorie felt his leg bump against another that was not his own. Then his head broke the surface, and he gasped for air. Dimly he registered a voice, but everything still felt too hazy for him to be able to understand what it was saying or even be sure that he was not imagining it. The thing around his chest and side tightened and then, through the fog that had swallowed the world, Lorie felt himself dragged jerkily through the water.

Lorie tried to help but by that point he was too exhausted to do much more than be pulled along in his rescuer's wake. Then he felt pebbles and wet earth beneath him, and with one final jerk that sent rocks tearing through his shirt and digging into the skin of his back, Lorie felt damp grass beneath his head, and he realized that he had been pulled at least partially free of the water.

The bands around his lungs seemed to have loosened somewhat, but they had not dissolved entirely and he coughed, trying to dislodge them. Lorie coughed again and again until he wa spitting water onto the grass beside him and was able to at last take a deep breath of the soft night air which played across his face.

"I told you that you couldn't trust that source of yours." The voice came from about a foot to Lorie's right. It was a tired voice, as though its owner still hadn't gotten his breath back after doing something exhausting, like running a marathon, or dragging a drowning assassin out of the Central Park boat pond. "You weren't kidding when you said you couldn't swim."

Lorie didn't bother opening his eyes. "What are you doing here?" he asked, his voice hoarse and raspy.

"That's really what you're going to start with? You're just lucky I was and even luckier that I took a lifeguarding class in college."

"I guess we're even now."

Xander let out a soft breath of amusement. "Guess so."

"Is that why you were following me around? Looking for an opportunity to get out of debt, or were you just looking to pick up a free scoop?" Lorie meant the comment as a joke, but another bout o coughing drove the humor from his voice.

"Something like that," Xander responded lightly all the same, as though he knew how Lorie had meant it. Then his voice turned serious. "Like I said, I don't trust Reynolds, and with him as your informant, I thought you might need someone watching your back."

Lorie sighed. "So I guess this is the part where you tell me, 'I told you so.'"

"No, I'll probably do that tomorrow, but for now this is the part where I tell you that I'm just glad that I was in time."

—From Book 3 of *Shadows of the Silver Towers* by A. B. Levinson

(NOW)

Alex woke in darkness. The sky was black, not a night sky tinged with moon and stars, but pure black, like the kind found in an unlit basement. That darkness was the second thing he noticed. The first was that he was lying on his back, and the third was the floor, shiny black tiles, the absolute black of onyx or coal, stretching away from him as far as his eyes could see in the gloom. For gloom it was. Despite the dark sky and black tiles, it was only gloomy, not pitch as it perhaps should have been.

Slowly, Alex used his elbows to push himself into a sitting position. He stared around, trying to orient himself in this strange unreality. Before him the blackness was broken by rectangles of light floating back and forth through the darkness. They seemed to flicker somehow, as though the color of the light was constantly changing, but they were far away and he couldn't make them out as much more than shapes of light.

He looked behind him and was surprised to see a chain-link fence topped with barbed wire standing tall only a few feet away. It seemed odd to him that in all of this strange, dreamlike space, there would be something as concrete and as ordinary as a fence. He turned to face it, curious. It really did seem like an ordinary fence, and when he reached out and ran his fingers across it, it felt ordinary enough. Not hot or cold, just metal of the sort you might find in a playground or around a parking lot, but beyond it there was nothing, no playground, no parking lot, no anything else. There was just blackness, unbroken even by a single floating light, and the smooth black of the floor tiles stretching out endlessly before him.

Slowly Alex stood, using the fence to help pull himself to his feet, and considered his next move. Climbing over the fence was out, the barbed wire at its top acting as more than enough of a deterrent for him. He could pick a direction and follow the fence one way or the other. It might lead him somewhere, but then again, it might not. He had no sense of how big this place was and, he realized, no reason to believe that it was limited by something as concrete as size in the first place. The fence stretched on and on as far as he could see in either direction. It might well go on like that for as far as he could follow it, and he had no way of knowing which way would lead him where he needed to go, wherever that was, and which would lead him into void. No, following the fence was also out, and that left only one option. He would head out across the floor and make for the lights; that way he would at least know that he was moving toward something. The idea of leaving the fence, the only concrete thing in this strange, nebulous un-world scared him a little, but just continuing to stand there wasn't going to do him any good. So Alex took a deep breath, pushed himself away from the fence, and set off into the darkness, searching for light and the shadow of a Raven.

As he drew closer, Alex realized that the rectangles of light were actually screens, like the sort found on flat-screen televisions, floating through the air. Curious, Alex sped up, coming to a halt just in front of the foremost screens and staring up at them. Clips were flickering across the screens, and he watched as a girl with wavy brown hair ran through a kitchen and out a side door into a small yard. On the next screen over, what appeared to be that same girl, but a few years older, leaned against a scraggly willow tree, her back to the screen and her face to a small cemetery. As he watched, she knelt, scooped up two rocks from between the willow's roots, and stepped forward to deposit one each on a pair of graves marked only by piled stones and temporary-looking small metal signs.

Then the scene changed, and he saw himself sitting with Raven, Ari, and Sean on the green. He and Ari were laughing. Sean was shaking a pencil at them in mock irritation, and Raven was smiling at them over the top of her book.

Then something flashing in his periphery caught Alex's eye, and he turned away from his past self to see the climactic fight scene from the movie they had gone to see on that fateful day, flashing across another screen. He blinked at it in surprise. After seeing that scene on the green, he'd assumed that what he was seeing were Raven's memories. By the time he'd met her she'd already started dying her hair, so it had taken him a few moments to recognize the child. However, the movie wasn't really a part of her life in the same way . . . or was it? Suddenly, remembering Lorie, he wasn't so sure.

As if in answer to his thought, a screen beyond it caught his eyes. On it a man with pale gray eyes and long sandy brown hair tied back in a ponytail stood, framed by the door of a hotel room. He was clearly furious, shouting something at a slim man with close-cut red-brown hair and hazel eyes who stood, arms crossed, staring calmly back at him. As Alex watched, the shorter man said something calmly, and the gray-eyed man froze, staring at the other in horrified consternation.

Alex was also frozen, staring up at the two incredulously. He knew the scene, of course, he did. In the months since that terrible day, he had read and reread every book of *Shadows of the Silver Towers*, seeking something that might have been understanding and might have been closure, and finding neither between its pages. Yes, he knew the scene, from the series' second novel. It was just that no part of the series had ever been televised or turned into a movie. Seeing those characters, Lorie and Xander, on the screen like this should have been impossible, for their likenesses existed only in the written word, in the illustrations drawn from those words, and in the reader's imagination. But then, Alex chided himself for a fool; that was just what this was after all—imagination. He was standing within Raven's mind, within her imagination and memory, and considering the way in which she had managed to quite literally bring Lorie to life. Was it any wonder that for Raven the two were mingled so completely that there was no longer any point to insisting on them as separate entities? This was how Raven saw the world, after all, a melding of fiction and fairytale, refracting reality and that reality itself a warped mirror of the human mind, twisted so that human truth reflected most brightly when looked at through the pages of that literary refraction. And he was standing in the middle of it.

Alex kept walking, eyes flicking from screen to screen as he passed through them, absorbing each image as he went on, trying as he did so to put aside the binaries of fiction and reality in order to see through them to the whole they created, the intertwining and interweaving of different story threads to create the person who was Raven. He was so absorbed in what the screens showed him that he didn't notice the house blooming out of the darkness until he was nearly upon it. He paused, examining it. The building was large, a mansion or a manor house, mixed oak paneling and white stone, its front supported by two tall white marble columns between which a set of matching marble steps led up to a curving oak door. There was nothing either to the right or to the left of the house, no path, no yard, no anything, just the blackness of the tile stretching away into eternity. There weren't even any screens for they came to an end abruptly a few yards from the front steps.

Slowly, almost hesitantly, Alex crossed the empty space between screens and steps. Then, taking a quick breath, he began to climb. The ascent had a dreamlike quality to it, wrapped as he was in this unreality, this non-world of blackness and dark tile. When he reached the top, he again hesitated for a moment before pushing open the door and stepping through.

What Alex saw within the house startled him more for its sheer normalcy than any abnormal site would have done. In front of him ran a long, broad hallway with a floor of polished dark wood. The hall was well lit with warm light shining down from two-pronged candle sconces affixed every few feet into white walls that were themselves bisected at regular intervals by thin dark wooden panels. A yard or two ahead to his left, the hall broadened into a rectangular alcove, at the back of which was a half-open door and at the front of which, and parallel to the hallway, sat the sort of desk often occupied by high school office secretaries. Its occupant was a slim, rather short, man who looked to be in his mid-twenties, with short red-brown hair, dressed in a white button-down, the sleeves of which were rolled up to above his elbows and the collar of which was open to reveal a flat Jewish star pendant made of twining slender silver wires hanging from a delicate silver chain around the man's neck.

Alex turned to look bemusedly from this incredibly ordinary site to the doorway behind him where an eternity of blackness stretched out, broken only by the flickering light of slowly drifting screens. Then he looked back at the man just as the man raised his head from whatever he had been writing and met Alex's eyes with his own intelligent hazel ones.

"Xander?" Alex asked. Maybe it was the amount of time he'd spent with Lorie or maybe it was the sheer impossibility of this un-world he was standing in, but Alex was far less surprised to meet this fictional entity then he might otherwise have been. In some ways, Alex felt that he should even have expected it.

Xander nodded calmly, apparently even less surprised to see Alex than Alex was to see him. "I am, and you are?"

"Alex, Alex Fine, I . . ." Alex trailed off, unsure how else he should identify himself, realizing as he spoke it that his name would mean nothing to the fictional entity set before him. Yet Xander seemed not even to have noticed Alex's sudden silence.

The moment he had spoken his name, Xander had lifted a giant leather-bound book from where it had sat on one side of the desk and had begun flipping through it, alternately running his forefinger down the page in front of him as though down a list and flipping through the book in search of some other page.

"Um." Alex said, unsure what he was supposed to be saying or doing.

Xander glanced up. "Close the door," he said briskly, "and then come over here."

Alex quickly obeyed, shooting one more glance out into the void before letting the door swing shut behind him and stepping up to Xander's desk. He peered down at the book and saw that Xander was indeed combing through lists, lists of names, to be precise, although the names themselves were written in such a curving and ornate handwriting that viewing them as he was upside down, Alex didn't have a chance to make them out before Xander was flipping to a new page. He continued for a few more moments before stopping with his finger halfway down a mostly empty page containing only five names. He tapped his finger lightly against a name, then looked up at Alex, his eyes shining with sudden interest.

"You're not fictional then?"

"Um, no," said Alex, a little taken aback by the bluntness of Xander's words.

"We've never had a nonfictional visitor before, not that we'd take most of them even if they'd come."

Alex rubbed self-consciously at the back of his head, unsure what to say to that.

"Not that you have anything to worry about in that regard," Xander said, keen gaze still fixed squarely on Alex, eyes burning with an intensity of interest that made Alex feel like shifting his weight from foot to foot. "You're cleared for almost everything around here."

"Cleared?"

Xander nodded. "It's my job to clear people after all, at least it is when I'm on guard duty. Those of us who serve as guards ensure that her mind stays in order and no one trespasses where they are not wanted."

"How do you do that? I mean couldn't someone just walk right past you?" Maybe if it had been Lorie sitting at that desk, things would have been different, but Alex knew that, quick on his feet though he might be, Xander was no one-man army.

At his question, a sly smile spread across Xander's face. "What makes you think that I'm alone out here?"

"I . . ."

"Guard room." Xander nodded in the direction of the half open door. "If anyone decides to try something with me or to try to go into an area where they don't belong, they'll find that it's not so easy as it looks."

"And what sort of people aren't welcome?"

"Some nonfictionals. That is, not people from nonfiction texts, but nonfiction people. She deserves her privacy and her secrets, and no magic user should be able to take that from her. Some fictionals, although then it's just a matter of where they can go and where they can't. The personalities of each of us she fully absorbs adds something to her sense of self, which is why it's important to make sure that those with toxic or poisonous mindsets, whether they be badly written characters or just the sort of antagonists that no one would ever enjoy, don't end up with free run of the place. Not, of course, that you have to worry about those sorts of limitations because, like I said, you're cleared for just about everything."

"I am?"

Xander nodded. "Yes, everything except dreams and subconscious thoughts, and nobody is cleared for those. She must really trust you." Now Alex thought that he understood the interest burning in Xander's eyes. It was the journalistic curiosity which served as one of his defining character traits. *What is it about you?* Xander's eyes seemed to ask him. *What did you do to make her trust you so?*

I don't know. Alex thought back at those eyes, remembering how easily he had believed that he meant nothing to Raven; a wave of guilt washed over him again. But was that entirely true? Did he really not know? Wasn't this just that same situation reversed, the memories that had flooded his head of all the time they had spent together, watched out for each other? Could that be the answer?

"So why are you here?" Xander spoke slowly, the curiosity strong in his tone.

"I have to find her."

Xander had never once yet used Raven's name, but there was only one her to whom he could have been referring, and so Alex felt no need to specify. "She's here, isn't she? I need to get her to come back with me."

"Oh, and why is that? Why is it exactly that you had to come all the way here to reach her?"

"I . . ." Alex hesitated, unsure how to summarize everything without going into unnecessary detail, then he shook his head. "If you don't know, then I don't know that it's mine to tell you. This is something that I need to talk about with her directly."

Xander frowned for a moment, chewing on his lower lip, then he nodded slowly. "Fair enough. I'll guide you to her as best I can." Then he turned and shouted over his shoulder "Leck!"

A moment later, a head poked around the door of what Xander had identified as the guard room. It belonged to a girl in her mid-teens with a freckled face, hazel eyes, and a long braid of sandy brown hair falling to her waist.

"What?"

"Would you mind watching the desk for a bit? Alex here needs a tour."

Leck raised her eyebrows, first at Xander then at Alex, withdrew her head to say something to the room's other occupants, then emerged fully, revealing that she was clad in a medieval-style teal-green leather tunic, brown trousers, and brown leather riding boots. There was a sword at her waist and a single golden bangle on her left wrist, made from three separate strands of golden wire and set with a single round bead of lapis lazuli. On the back of her left hand glowed a gold crescent moon. Her nails, where they rested against the pommel of her sword, were rather longer and sharper than those of an ordinary human. Alex suddenly understood very well what Xander meant when he said those who wished to break the rules of this place would have trouble doing so. He knew this girl; although, unlike the way in which he had half expected Xander, he'd never dreamed to one day see her in the flesh. This was Leck, one of the main characters of the fantasy series *The Order of the Blade*. Her nails did not look human because they, like the rest of her, were as much a dragon as they were anything else, and if she chose now to wear a mostly human skin, it was just that—a choice.

Xander stood, and Leck took his now empty seat at the entrance desk. Xander walked out from behind it and gestured for Alex to follow him.

"Come on. This way."

They began to walk down the hallway, Alex glancing around himself, taking it all in, and Xander frowning slightly and looking pensive. A few yards down the hallway they passed a mirror mounted on the wall, made of thick glass and cut in the size and shape of a round-topped doorway. Alex glanced at it, then did a double take, turning to stop and stare. It wasn't that his reflection was missing—it was there all right, dressed in the same jeans and T-shirt he had put on that morning. No, what was strange was what was behind his reflection: a room, rounded and filled with bookshelves with a couple of armchairs at its center. Alex glanced wildly behind himself, backing up until his shoulders hit the hard, unyielding surface of the wall. It looked just the same as it had when he entered the hallway, and the way it felt matched exactly what his eyes were showing him. Yet, when he turned back to the mirror, there was the room of books reflected precisely where his fingers told him it wasn't.

Xander had come to a halt as well and was now trying (and failing) to muffle his amusement at the look on Alex's face. Alex didn't have to guess what sort of look he was making, since he could see it stamped right across his reflection, reflected right on top of a room that did not exist. Still trying to muffle his laughter behind one hand, Xander used his other hand to gesture Alex toward the mirror. Hesitantly, Alex stepped up to it and rested his hand upon it. It was cool to the touch but no more than he would expect from glass, and he was about to pull his hand away and demand an explanation when he felt the mirror's surface soften and give way under his fingers. He felt them sink into the glass and through it until there was nothing but air around them, and they were no longer reflected in the mirror but instead part of the room beyond.

"What the hell!"

"Th-through the looking glass," Xander managed to say between bouts of laughter. "It was a very formative work for her."

Alex blinked at him, then at the mirror. Slowly, he pulled his hand out again, breathing a sigh of relief when he felt it come free of the glass.

"So that's a door then?"

Xander nodded, eyes still bright with amusement.

They continued walking until they reached a crossroads. Xander hesitated for only a moment before taking the leftward fork. As they went, they would occasionally pass other people moving through the halls. Some ignored them altogether, some greeted Xander, and a few shot curious glances in Alex's direction. For his part, all Alex could do was to stare fixedly first at one person then at another, trying to place in which fictional work each of them belonged. They passed more of the mirrored doors, most of them also leading into small libraries of various shapes, and one door that was not a mirror but an actual door, made of dark wood and set with a heavy round metal handle. They also passed through several more intersections, and at each Xander would pause for a little longer before choosing a direction.

They had just started moving again, after a particularly long pause, when Xander came to an abrupt halt and swore loudly.

"What?" Alex asked, glancing around, and then he saw it too. There was a mirror-door on his right, and its size and shape and the room beyond it all looked exactly like the first mirror-door that they had passed, the one he'd stuck his hand into. No, it didn't look like that mirrored door, unless he was very much mistaken; it *was* that mirrored door. Thus far at least, all of the library rooms had looked different and distinctive, but this one looked identical to that first one, down to the location of the two armchairs.

"Is that?"

"It is." Xander sighed heavily.

"But how?"

"The hallways are moving. It's why I keep stopping at the intersections. I keep trying to feel where she is, and I can, but it's one thing to feel her and another thing to get to her if she doesn't want to be gotten to."

"Feel her?" Alex frowned. There wasn't anything supernatural in *Shadows of the Silver Towers*. Xander shouldn't have been able to feel anything less natural than a breeze.

"Yeah. We all can. She's the heart of this place after all, but that also means it responds to her emotions, and right now she's not really in the mood for visitors. That's why I said I would do my best, but I didn't promise you anything."

"Oh . . ." Alex frowned, looking at the ground. "Does that mean she doesn't want to see me?"

Xander shrugged. "Perhaps, but I doubt it. If she really didn't want you here, you wouldn't have the sort of clearance that you do. There's a good chance she doesn't even know you're here, since even in this place she isn't omniscient."

"She's not?"

"No." Xander shook his head. "I suppose she could be if she wanted to be, but she wanted us to be people, not puppets or play things, and for us to be people to her she can't be any more than any of us."

"Oh." Alex stood there just digesting that for a moment. "So then, if this place is moving, how do we find her?"

"We keep looking."

So they did, passing through hall after hall and by mirror after mirror. Sometimes they passed the first mirrored door again, and sometimes they passed the lone wooden door, although that one was always just past the left fork of the same intersection, and Alex was starting to get the distinct impression that, unlike the rest of the place, it wasn't moving. As they passed it for a fifth time, Alex put out a hand and tapped Xander on the shoulder.

"What?"

"What about this door? It doesn't look like it's moving."

Xander frowned and shook his head. "Not that way. I don't have the clearance for that door."

"Do I?"

Xander blinked at him for a minute. Then his eyes widened as a slow smile spread across his face. "You do, don't you? And while it's not the most pleasant idea, it certainly isn't the worst one either."

"Not the most pleasant?"

"It's not a pleasant door."

"What the fuck does that mean?"

Xander just smiled and shook his head.

Shrugging, Alex stepped toward it, grabbing the ring and pulling it open. The curve of the metal felt cool and heavy against his hand, but the door slid open easily enough. In front of him was blackness, not the total blackness of the unreality beyond the walls of the house, but a more normal blackness, like a poorly lit room. In front of him, Alex could just make out a black metal spiral staircase and beyond it, down in the darkness, a faintly pulsing blue-green light. He turned, glancing back once more at Xander and the brightly lit hallway.

"Good luck." Xander said it quietly. "And take care of her."

Alex nodded. "I will."

Alex's feet clinked faintly against the metal of the spiral staircase as he descended slowly, one hand gripping the banister. As he went, he tried to make out the details of the room he was descending into, and slowly they began to materialize out of the darkness, what few there were anyway. The room was round, and its floor and walls were made of yellowed canvas, as though part of a circus tent. A little bit of yellow light seemed to glow from the center of the floor, like the last dying gasps of a reverse spotlight, one that shone from below instead of above. There was another source of light in the room as well, the blues and greens that he had glimpsed from above. It was coming, he soon saw, from the one wall that was not made out of canvas. Descending the final step, Alex turned to gaze at it. The wall looked like some translucent, porous thing. It rippled and rolled with shapes of dark blue and sea green, grays and navies, olive drab, and black.

Some bits of it were beautiful, but the overall impression he got was more of repulsion than of beauty. There was something deeply wrong about it. Still, it mesmerized him somehow. Perhaps it was the way it seemed to pulsate, perhaps it was the way the shapes moved and twisted within it, but Alex felt himself drawn toward it until he stood right before it. Curious about its strange rippling movement and about what that could mean for its substance, Alex extended a hand, his fingers brushing against it. He had wondered what it would feel like, but he never got the chance to find out.

Before his body could so much as absorb the sensation of fingers meeting wall, another, far more powerful sensation washed over him, blotting out every other thought and feeling. Pain. Pain that ripped through his head with a force he had never dreamed of, pain that wracked his entire body. A single wave of it, long and lasting and never easing, just piling on, continuing until he felt like his mind, his very essence, was shattering, breaking apart under the agony of it. He thought he screamed but he wasn't sure if any noise actually left his lips. His face was screwed up against the dim light that suddenly burned far too brightly, stabbing into his eyes. Then suddenly there was another sensation, a tug on the back of his shirt, an oath from behind him, and the pain was ebbing away just like that.

Alex fell to his knees, panting and gasping and shaking as the last of the agony rolled off of him, leaving him feeling muddled and disoriented but blissfully pain-free.

"What the hell were you thinking?"

The voice behind him sounded irritated, and it was wonderfully familiar. Alex spun half around on his knees, eyes blinking rapidly to clear themselves of tears he hadn't even remembered forming, and he took relieved note of the fact that they seemed to be registering light properly again.

"Raven!"

It was Raven. She was standing just behind him, arms crossed, head tilted to one side as she glared down at him.

"Alex?" The irritation melted off of her, washed away by utter surprise and confusion. "What? How? What are you doing here?"

Quickly, Alex scrambled to his feet. "I . . ." He faltered, trying to put his thoughts back into some semblance of order after the chaos that the pain had left them in. The pain.

"What was that?"

"That"—Raven's face clouded again, and she stepped past him to stand before the wall, eyeing it calmly—"was a migraine."

"A . . . , wait, what?"

"You're in my mind now, Alex. That means everything else is in here too, my hopes, and dreams and, yes, my fears and pain as well. The migraines themselves are not simply products of my imagination but rather the products of my neural network, but then"—she turned back toward him—"so is the rest of this place, and so are all my thoughts and feelings. The mind and body are not so separate as some claim them to be. So yes"—she nodded back over her shoulder at the wall behind her—"this is a migraine."

"And they're like that, all the time?"

"No, not always, thank God! That's only what they're like at their very worst, but they do get there from time to time."

"And how, how long do they last like that?"

"It depends, but the longest I've ever had to deal with them on that level was eight hours."

"Eight hours!" Alex licked suddenly dry lips. "Your head feels like that for eight hours?"

"It can."

Alex shook his head in horror. He had only been in contact with the wall for a few moments, and he'd already felt as though his very mind were splitting apart. To feel like that for eight consecutive hours . . . ?

Before he could pursue that line of questioning any further, however, Raven took a step toward him, her eyes narrowing.

"What are you doing here, Alex?" she repeated, slight suspicion in her tone. And he felt their last meeting crash down between them, and he remembered anew what he had said and how he had acted toward her.

"I came to apologize." He said it softly.

"Apologize?" There was surprise in her voice.

"Yeah . . . After everything that happened . . . Everything you did . . . The way I acted . . ." He shook his head. "Lorie told me everything, the risks you were willing to take for us, and I was still such a jerk . . . but I thought . . . when you said that you picked us—picked me—because I was a sleeper, I thought you meant that that was the only reason you stayed around us, around me, that I didn't mean anything else to you . . ."

Raven's eyes widened. She looked genuinely stricken. "Alex, that's not . . . You should know that I . . . that your . . ." She stumbled to a halt, shaking her head in frustration. "Stupid language. There's just no way to say some things without sounding like . . ." She shook her head again and sighed. "That *is* why I picked you. I meant what I said. I was curious. I know the way I see the world isn't, well, typical. I've always wondered if the way I think, whether that's because of my magic. I always wondered if another mage would be more, well, more like me." As she spoke, Raven's expression shifted, making her seem both younger and more vulnerable then she had ever seemed to Alex before, and he wanted desperately to say something to reassure her, that she was not in fact, alone. Before he could find the right words, however, she continued talking.

"That's what I wondered, when I met you, wondered if your thoughts were more, well, what's seen as normal, or whether they would be more like mine."

I could have told you that. Alex thought. *I could have told you that they were like yours.* There were many words that Alex would use to describe himself, bookworm, nerd, quick-witted, empathetic, but neurotypical had never been among them.

"So, you really did always know then? That you were a mage?"

She nodded. "The sight, like I said. Why else do you think I picked the name Raven?"

He blinked, surprised at that. He had known, of course, that she had picked the name out for herself, discarding the one she'd been given at birth for one that she felt suited her better. He had not, however, realized that her choice of a new name had held any significance beyond that.

She smiled a little at his obvious confusion. "Yes, I chose to name myself for the birds long connected with the power of sight, and I chose my hair color to match my new name."

"So all this time you could've just done magic?" he demanded.

She shook her head. "Not like that, not anything I could prove, not really. I could see, of course, and sometimes the visions were clear. But sometimes they weren't, at least not until after they were already on their way to becoming true."

"Why though?"

"Because, in a sense, I wasn't fully awake either. I knew magic was real, knew that what I saw in dreams kept coming true. Yet there was still some level of doubt, something that I couldn't quite push past until the moment I saw another person working magic in front of me."

"That moment in the tunnel?"

"Exactly."

"So before that, all you could do was seeing and luck stuff?"

"And sensing other mages."

"Um, right. And that's how you found me . . ."

She nodded. "I was curious." Raven said it again, "But that was only why I picked you, why I decided to start talking to you, not why I kept talking to you. That was because . . ." She trailed away again, letting out a slight snort of frustration.

"Because?"

"As much as I love words, this language can be incredibly lacking sometimes." She shook her head again. "The way you're always looking out for me, the way you always see me, see what's going on with me. You notice when I'm on the outside of things, you pick up on my tells for a migraine onset faster than anyone I've ever met, even my aunt. You mentioned Lorie before, so I'm guessing you were the one who figured out we switched places."

Alex nodded slowly.

"I should have realized you would." She smiled slightly. "What I'm trying to say is . . ." She took a breath, staring fixedly down at her sandals. "What I'm trying to say is love but not 'in love.' Caring, but not that sort of caring. But there just aren't words to say it without it sounding like I mean the other thing, and I definitely don't but I want to say it anyway because . . ."

"Yeah, same here."

Raven's breath caught in her throat, and she looked up quickly so that their eyes met.

"I didn't know how to say it either, but I know what you're trying to say because I feel the same way."

Alex took a quick step forward and wrapped his arms around Raven.

She stood there for a second, just blinking up at him, then she wrapped her arms around him tightly, returning the embrace.

Alex could feel tears in his eyes, rolling downward and across his cheeks. She was here, she was really here, after all those months she was really, truly, finally here. This wasn't someone else walking around in Raven's familiar form. No, the person hugging him back was truly her. The relief of having her so close again was enough to double the speed of his tears.

"You mean the world to me Alex." She said it softly.

"You too."

They were silent for a little while after that, just holding each other for the comfort it brought both of them.

At last they separated. Alex wiped his eyes with the back of one hand and said, "I didn't just come here to apologize though."

"Oh?"

"I came to ask you to come back with me. Lorie said you're probably the only one who can undo whatever it is you did to end up in here, so . . ."

His voice trailed away as he noticed the sudden tension in her shoulders.

"Raven?"

She took a step away from him, shaking her head.

"No."

He stared at her. "No?"

She shook her head again. "No."

Fear began to rise in him. Did she mean that there was no way out? That the two of them were stuck there forever? That . . . His eyes narrowed. He knew Raven, and her expression now.

"Do you mean that you can't or that you won't?"

"I . . ." She glanced away. "It's better here."

"Raven . . ." His tone softened and he reached out, hesitating for a moment before resting a hand on her arm. "You can't stay in here forever."

"Why not?" She made no move, either to look up at him or to push his hand away.

"Because this"—he gestured around them at the canvas walls and the staircase and the pulsing light of the migraine behind him—"this isn't really living."

She shifted a little at that, and when she spoke again there was annoyed impatience in her tone.

"Don't tell me you're going to go off on one of those speeches about how normal life matters more than stories."

The thought was so amusing that, despite his worries for her, he almost laughed. "Hey, this is me, remember? I'd never say something that's stupid."

"Then?"

He hesitated for a moment, searching for the words, the words that could make her abandon this land of fiction and safety for the boring uncertainty and pain of reality. His thoughts returned to New York, to the ordinary day at the movies they'd been having before everything went wrong, and then to Lorie and to the screens floating in the nothingness beyond the front doors, and to what he'd seen on them.

At last he said, "They both matter, stories and normal life, they're both real and they're both part of you, right? But if you stay here, they both end."

At that she looked up at him and he saw uncertainty in her eyes. "What do you mean?"

"This place, it's everything you already are and know, right? Then there won't be any new stories here, and there won't be your story, and you need both, the books you read and your life, your story, so please . . ."

She looked away again, taking in the space along with his words. For several long moments she was silent, considering; then, at last, she spoke, her voice soft but determined.

"A word is dead when it is said, some say. I say it has just begun to live that day."

He breathed out, relief rising in him as he recognized the quote. "You can't say much from in here."

She shook her head, her strange, bird-black eyes, once again meeting his, and there was determination in them too.

"No, I can't."

He took a tentative step closer. "So can you?"

"Can I?"

"Undo it."

"I think so . . ." She nodded as she said it, but there was still uncertainty in her eyes. For a moment they flicked over his shoulder to the pulsing light of the migraine and he understood, going back to reality would mean going back to that pain too, on top of everything else. He felt the memory of it under his skin and, inwardly, he shuddered at it, but even with that waiting for her, she couldn't stay here, and they both knew it.

Raven took a breath, squaring her shoulders against the idea of once more facing the outside world. Then, slowly, she nodded.

Much as he wanted to, he couldn't do anything about the pain, but at least he could make sure she didn't have to face it alone, that neither one of them needed to face things alone.

He smiled at her and rested his hand against her arm for a moment.

"Are you ready?"

She breathed in, held it for a moment, then breathed out, before smiling back.

"Ready."

Raven extended her hand and Alex took it.

ABOUT THE AUTHOR

S. Judith Bernstein (SJ) is a fantasy author and lifelong lover of all things magical. They graduated from Mount Holyoke College in 2019 and now live in Boston with their found family of roommates and their cat Prospero. In Shadowed Dreams is their debut novella. Their next upcoming release is The Blood of Pendragon, an epic fantasy queering of the Legend of King Arthur.

To get a sneak peak of their next release, find out when pre-orders will be available, keep up with what project they will be working on next and more, sign up for their email list at

https://www.trickstercatpublishing.com

Made in United States
North Haven, CT
24 March 2023

34516883R00075